THE LINCOLN LIBRARY OF SPORTS CHAMPIONS

EIGHTH EDITION

THE
LINCOLN
LIBRARY Cleveland, Ohio

The Lincoln Library of Sports Champions, Eighth Edition

For more information contact: The Lincoln Library Press, 812 Huron Road E, Ste 401, Cleveland, Ohio 44115–1172 Or visit our web site at: www.TheLincolnLibrary.com

The Lincoln Library Press is an imprint of, and The Lincoln Library owl is a trademark of, Eastword Publications Development, Inc., Cleveland, Ohio.

Although every effort has been made to ensure the accuracy of the information contained herein, The Lincoln Library Press does not guarantee the accuracy of the data. Errors submitted to and verified by the publisher will be corrected in future editions.

Cataloging-in-Publication Data

The Lincoln library of sports champions. — 8th ed.
Cleveland, Ohio : Lincoln Library, c2007.
        14 v.

        Includes bibliographical references and index.

        Summary: Presents brief, alphabetically arranged biographies of 300 great sports personalities, past and present, from around the world. Some of the new sports included in this edition are curling, lacrosse, and snowboarding. Features a table of contents arranged by sport, indexes by gender, nationality, and historic era.

        ISBN-13: 978-0-912168-25-8 (set)
        ISBN-10: 0-912168-25-0 (set)

        1. Athletes—Biography—Encyclopedias, Juvenile.
[1. Athletes—Encyclopedias. 2. Sports—Encyclopedias.]
I. Gall, Timothy L.

GV697.A1 L56 2007
796.0922—dc22

                                2006907320

Printed in China
by Kings Time Printing Press, Ltd.

10 9 8 7 6 5 4 3 2 1

The Lincoln Library Press,
inspiring independent inquisitive minds,
is named for Abraham Lincoln,
America's foremost autodidact.

CONTENTS

Volume 5

Fleming, Peggy

Peggy Fleming (1948–   ), figure skater, was born in San Jose, California. She began skating at the age of 9 and by 1960 had won the Pacific Coast juvenile figure-skating championship. In 1961, she won the Pacific Coast novice ladies' championship, and at 15 gained her first women's national senior title. At the 1964 Winter Olympics in Innsbruck, Austria, Peggy placed sixth in figure-skating competition. In 1965, Peggy's family moved to Colorado Springs, Colorado, where she came under the coaching guidance of Carlo Fassi. By the next year she had won her first of three consecutive international championships. She also won the North American title. The national champion from 1964 to 1968, Peggy won the only gold medal for the United States at the 1968 Winter Olympics at Grenoble, France. She dazzled the

judges with her spectacular and ballet-like routines, including the "spread-eagle double-axel spread-eagle." At the end of the 1967–68 season, Peggy retired from amateur competition. She later appeared with the Ice Follies. Fleming became an analyst for televised skating events, including the Winter Olympics.

On February 15, 1961, tragedy struck the United States Olympic skating team. A plane crashed in Belgium, killing 18 top U.S. figure skaters and coaches. After that sad event, it took several years to find and train promising new athletes to serve as America's skaters. Even then, the resulting U.S. teams were weak since there were no experienced people to strengthen the skaters and weld them together as a team. The nation that had won 21 world figure-skating championships in the 13 years before the crash could not muster a single winner afterward. And then, a 5-foot, 3-inch, 109-pound brunette named Peggy Fleming entered the scene.

Peggy Fleming was the only American to stand this high on the winner's pedestal during the 1968 Winter Olympics. She won the gold medal for figure skating.

Fleming, Peggy

Redeeming the Skating Legacy

In 1966, during the world figure-skating championships in Davos, Switzerland, the graceful 17-year-old glided over the ice—effortlessly spinning, jumping, and performing intricate movements until the audience leaped to its feet in pleasure. The young American captured the judges' esteem as well, for she was awarded the world championship title, the first in five years for the United States.

Yet the thrill of her victory was short. A few hours after the event, Peggy Fleming learned that her father, the person most responsible for her success, had died of a heart attack.

Unfortunately, Albert Fleming did not see his daughter skate on to greater honors, or capture the only gold medal awarded to an American at the 1968 Winter Olympics. But he had faith that she would make it to the top. He had seen her potential when she was still a child and had worked hard to create in her the desire to become a world champion.

The Early Years

Peggy Gale Fleming was born July 27, 1948, in San Jose, California, the second of four daughters. At 9, she was first introduced to the world of ice skating after a family move to Cleveland, Ohio.

"She took to skating right away," one of her younger sisters recalled. "She started skating as though she had been at it for a long time."

Albert Fleming encouraged his daughter to develop her talent by practicing on the ice. After another family move back to California, young Peggy Fleming began entering competitions. A year later, she won her first title, the Pacific Coast juvenile figure-skating championship. The years following held many other championships for her—the Pacific Coast novice ladies' championship (1961), second place in the national novice ladies' championship (1962), the Pacific Coast senior ladies' title (1963), and her first women's national senior title (1964).

The last victory gave her an entry into the U.S. Olympic team, and at the 1964 Winter Olympics, Peggy Fleming placed sixth in the figure-skating competition. This was an amazing feat for a 15-year-old girl attending her first world meet.

On the Rise

Peggy Fleming continued her rise, winning new competitions and defending past titles. In March 1965, at the international figure-skating championships at Broadmoor World Arena, Colorado Springs, Peggy Fleming placed third. Her father realized that she could have done even better but for the high altitude of the area. Unused to the thin air, she tired easily. Albert Fleming also knew the next year's competition was to be held in Davos, Switzerland—also in a high altitude.

A measure of a family's love and faith can often be found in the sacrifices it makes for its own. The Fleming family is a good example. There is a great financial burden in reaching a championship. Lessons, rink-time rental, travel, and costume expenses are barriers that must be overcome. But Peggy Fleming was lucky.

Never well-off, the entire family worked hard so she could have every chance to reach for the top. Her mother made all her skating costumes. Her father often worked double shifts to help pay the extra bills. The family was even willing to be uprooted if it became necessary to her career.

Albert Fleming saw his daughter's need for high-altitude practice and further coaching. And he decided to give her that chance. In June 1965, he found a new job as a newspaper pressman in Colorado Springs.

Peggy Fleming spent the next year practicing in the Broadmoor Arena under the guidance of Carlo Fassi, former European men's skating champion. Her years of grueling five-hour-a-day workouts, her practice to build thin-air

Fleming, Peggy

Career Highlights

Won the Pacific Coast novice ladies championship in 1960 at age 12

Captured her first women's senior title at age 15

Emerged as the U.S. national champion for five consecutive years (1964–68)

Three-time world champion (1966–68)

Won an Olympic gold medal at the 1968 Olympics in Grenoble, France

stamina, and the extra coaching from Fassi paid off in Davos. The international figure-skating title (1966) was hers.

With her second Olympic competition in sight, Peggy warmed up by capturing new crowns and defending old ones. She was no longer a novice to world competition after winning five national skating championships and two world titles. Her skating had been described as "flawless" and "superb" by judges. She was in good health, 19 years old, and she was ready.

Looking like she is about to take a nosedive into the ice, Peggy practices before the 1968 Winter Olympics at Grenoble, France.

A Skater Unlike Any Other

What set Peggy Fleming apart from other skaters was not just her technical skill—although some experts at the time doubted that she could be matched. Nor was it her mature dedication to her career. It was something different—something unique in her style.

Dick Button, perhaps the greatest male skater in history, said of her, "She is an exquisite skater,

"The first thing is to love your sport. Never do it to please someone else. It has to be yours."

—Peggy Fleming, on her love of ice skating

Getting a warm welcome at home in Colorado after winning a gold medal at the 1968 Winter Olympics, Peggy receives a flower from a fan.

lyrically expressive and technically fine....She is not a fiery skater, and she shouldn't be made to be. With some skaters there is a lot of fuss and feathers, but nothing is happening. With Peggy, there's no fuss and feathers, and a great deal is happening."

This fluidity of motion through such special routines as the "spread-eagle double-axel spread-eagle"—which no other woman in international competition had been able to master—added to her precise tracing of the extremely difficult school figures (variations on figure eights). Her performance caused one Olympic official at the time to call her "the best skater there has ever been."

After receiving the Olympic gold medal, she went on to win yet another world championship—her third and last.

A New Career On Ice

On March 2, 1968, Peggy Fleming announced her retirement from amateur competition. The financial strain had been a hard one for her mother and sisters—and there

were no more titles to conquer. In April, she announced that she had signed a contract with Bob Banner Associates, television producers. And Peggy then appeared in her own television specials and as a guest star for the Ice Follies. Her competitive career lasted less than 10 years and she was still a teenager when she retired. But those years were spent in single-minded determination to get to the top. Peggy Fleming had help along the way, but the loneliness and pain of constant practice were hers alone. Hers, too, was the final test before the judges. But everyone shared the product of her efforts—perhaps the most beautiful skating the world has ever seen.

Further Study

BOOKS

Cantwell, Lois and Pohla Smith. *Women Winners: Then and Now.* New York, NY: Rosen Publishing Group, 2003.

Ditchfield, Christin. *Top 10 American Women's Gold Medalists.* Springfield, NJ: Enslow Publishing, 2000.

Tabby, Abigail. *Grace on Ice: Peggy Fleming, Dorothy Hamill, Michelle Kwan.* New York, NY: Golden Books, 2001.

WEB SITES

"Peggy Fleming, "*Sports Illustrated Women.* Online at www.sportsillustrated.cnn.com/siforwomen/top_100/19/ (October 2006)

"Peggy Fleming," *United States Olympic Team.* Online at www.olympic-usa.org/26_13370.htm (October 2006)

⊚Force, John

John Force (1949–   ), drag racer, was born in Bell Gardens, California. He competed in 66 races without winning, but he didn't give up. No other driver has been named to the Auto Racing All-American Team as often as Force (11 times). He is the winningest driver in drag racing history with 122 career victories as of

November 2006. Force won ten consecutive National Hot Rod Association (NHRA) Funny Car Championships (1993–2002). He collected a record 14 NHRA PowerADE Championships during his career. Force held the Funny Car record for both the fastest quarter-mile time (4.665 seconds) and the fastest overall speed (333.58 mph).

John Force was 38 years old in 1987. He had been competing in drag races since 1978. He had raced 66 times and not won a race. He came in second nine times in a row and was beginning to wonder if he would ever win a race.

John Force was born May 4, 1949, in Bell Gardens, California. He had polio as a child. Polio is a crippling disease that has now been eliminated by a vaccine. Polio left Force with one leg slightly shorter than the other. John Force is not the type of person to get discouraged or to give up, even when he has setbacks. He didn't let the effects of polio keep him from being active. He played quarterback for the Bell Gardens High School football team. The team lost 27

games in a row, but Force never thought about giving up football. He took the field each season with dedication.

Even as a teenager, John Force loved to drive fast. The first time a policeman stopped him for speeding in Downey, California, Force was only 14 years old.

John Force wanted to drive race cars. It is an expensive activity. To earn money, he worked driving an 18-wheel truck, hauling cargo long distances. John Force has an outgoing personality. A truck-driving school hired him to star in their commercials. He started racing in 1974. For the next 12 years, he entered drag race after drag race and he was always on a tight budget. He and his mechanics would sleep six to

a motel room when they traveled to races. Force remembers those years when money was tight, recalling that he sometimes slept in a truck in his brother's driveway between races.

Almost every weekend, he climbed into the tiny cockpit of his Funny Car. A Funny Car is sometimes called a rocket on wheels. Force often finished second, but he didn't finish first.

Top Fuel Dragsters and Funny Cars are the two fastest categories of drag racing. Drag races take place on a one-quarter mile track in front of thousands of spectators. The rear tires on the Funny Cars are called slicks because they have no treads. Just before the race, the tires are spun to heat them up. Warm tires have better traction on

Force takes off from the line in his Funny Car.

the track. In each drag race, two cars line up at the starting line. The drivers watch a series of lights on a pole, called a "Christmas tree." The lights move from amber to the final green. When they see the green light, both drivers hit the throttle. The cars take off, traveling about 300 miles per hour. There are many accidents. Crashes are often fiery because of the fuel. Force has crashed and burned many times. Most drag racers have an aggressive, fearless attitude. "It's all reflexes. If you think, you lose," Force says.

Force's car, a Castrol GTX Ford Mustang, goes from zero to 100 in less than a second. "The idea of this car isn't to dash it through four hours of a circle race, it's to push it to the limit," explains Force. "If I can stay just this side of breaking, I can win the race."

Force joined the NHRA Series in 1978, but failed for nearly ten years to win even one event. Force borrowed money to make his driving dream a reality. In 1985, Force teamed with Austin Coil, a respected crew chief, to achieve his goal of winning an NHRA title.

Finally, in 1987, at the age of 38, he captured the elusive victory at Le Grandnational in Montreal, Canada. The breakthrough victory started Force on a winning streak. Three years later, in 1990, he won his first NHRA Championship. He repeated the feat the following season and finished second overall in the standings in 1992. What would follow was a run of success unparalleled in professional sports.

Force reclaimed the NHRA title in 1993 while driving for Team Castrol. He then went on to retain the championship for an amazing ten straight years (1993–2002). The streak of ten consecutive championships is the best in sports history, including team sports. (The Boston Celtics of the NBA won eight consecutive titles, the closest to Force's record.)

John's 1996 season stands out as one of the greatest in racing history. He won 13 races, appeared in 16 final rounds, and won 65 elimination rounds en route to the title. All are single-season NHRA records. For his efforts, Force was selected as Driver of the Year for all American motor racing. He became the first—and only—drag racer ever to earn such an honor.

John Force is respected in the racing world and his outgoing personality helps to attract fans to the sport of drag racing. He loves Elvis Presley, and even keeps a picture of Elvis taped to his dashboard. Force also loves the fans, and dreams of having throngs of followers, just like Elvis did.

Force and his wife, Laurie, have four daughters: Adria, Ashley (also a drag racer), Brittany, and Courtney. The entire Force family is often seen at the track when John Force is racing.

Bob Frey, NHRA race announcer and statistician, remarked, "John Force has done it all and has probably done more to elevate the image of our sport than anyone else. He is, easily, the most popular driver of all time and his on-track accomplishments speak for themselves."

Further Study

Bledsoe, Glen and Karen Bledsoe. *The World's Fastest Dragsters.* Mankato, MN: Capstone, 2003.

Cockerham, Paul W. *Drag Racing.* Philadelphia: Chelsea House, 1997.

John Force Racing. Online at www.johnforceracing.com/ (October 2006)

⚾ Ford, Whitey

Whitey (Edward) Ford (1928–), baseball player, was born in a Manhattan tenement district of New York City. Ford played first base and pitched for a neighborhood sandlot team and Manhattan High School of Aviation Trades. Shortly after graduating from high school in 1946, Ford signed a contract with the New York Yankees. An excellent pitcher in the minor leagues, Ford was brought up to the Yankees during the 1950 season. With 25 victories, four losses, and an earned-run average (ERA) of 3.21 in 1961, Ford was chosen the Cy Young Award winner as the outstanding pitcher in the major leagues. Whitey Ford ended his big-league career in 1967 with a lifetime won-lost record of 236 and 106; a winning percentage of .690,

which ranks among the top five all-time for pitchers with more than 200 career victories; and an ERA of 2.74. After retiring as a player, he served as a minor league and major league pitching coach for the Yankees. Ford was inducted into the Baseball Hall of Fame in 1974.

More than any other player of his time, Whitey Ford perhaps deserves to be known as baseball's "thinking-man's pitcher."

Ford, the famous southpaw of the New York Yankees, achieved a lifetime won-lost mark of 236–106. He earned his reputation as the "money" pitcher for the great Yankee teams of the 1950s and 1960s. And what he may have lacked in overpowering speed, Ford made up in cleverness, style, and a mixed selection of curves and offspeed pitches.

Edward Charles "Whitey" Ford was one of those lucky athletes who got to play in the city where he was born and reared. Ford was born October 21, 1928, in New York City. He grew up in a tenement in Manhattan and began his baseball career as a first baseman and pitcher on the city sandlots.

Posting 25 victories in 1961, Whitey Ford won the American League Cy Young Award as the outstanding pitcher of the year.

Ford, Whitey

Ford was small for an athlete, growing to only 5 feet, 10 inches, and 175 pounds. But the New York Yankees liked what they saw of him at the Manhattan High School of Aviation Trades and offered him a contract. He pitched brilliantly in the minors and was an immediate sensation when he was brought up to the Yankees in 1950. Though the season was half over, Ford still won nine games and lost only one.

He got to start a game in the World Series, too, in that rookie season, and held the Philadelphia Phillies scoreless for 8⅔ innings as he chalked up a victory.

Before his career was over, Ford set World Series records for the most victories (10) and consecutive scoreless innings (33⅔). His overall career won-lost percentage of .690 ranked second in major league history.

The Yankee Ace

Oddly enough, Ford won 20 games only twice during his 16-year career—in 1961, when his record was 25–4; and in 1963, when his record was 24–7. This was because Yankee manager Casey Stengel used him as a "super spot starter" (not as a pitcher in the regular rotation, but as a starter in key games) during the 1950s.

But when Ralph Houk took over as the Yankees' manager in the early 1960s, Whitey Ford became the unquestioned ace of the team. He increased his number of starts by almost 10 games per season. Under Houk, Ford proved that he could pitch as well as ever on a regular four-day rotation. In five straight seasons from 1960 through 1964, he pitched over 200 innings per year.

After breaking into baseball with such a splash in 1950, Ford spent two years in the military service. Then he came back in 1953 to pick up where he had left off. In that year, his record was 18–6.

After winning 16 of 24 games in 1954—the year the Yankees lost the pennant—Whitey came back in 1955 to lead the American League in victories with 18 games. The same year, he won two of three World Series games the Yankees were able to take from the Brooklyn Dodgers.

In 1956, Ford got even closer to his first 20-win season, by winning 19 and losing only six for a .760 percentage—again tops in the league. His 2.47 earned-run average also led all American League pitchers that year.

A shoulder injury in 1957 limited Ford to only 24 games and

Ford, Whitey

an 11–5 mark. But he came back strong in 1958 to lead the league once again in earned-run average (2.01) while chalking up a 14–7 record.

Two rather average seasons in 1959 and 1960 made many believe that Ford, like Casey Stengel, was nearing the end of a glorious era. But with Houk as the Yankees' manager in 1961, Whitey suddenly "re-blossomed" at the ripe age of 33 and completed his first 20-win season.

Yankee Glory

It was in 1961 that Mickey Mantle and Roger Maris combined for 115 home runs. And while Ford led the league in games started (39), it was also the season a roly-poly Puerto Rican relief pitcher named Luis Arroyo became famous as the Yankees' ace reliever. Ford won his career high of 25 games that year, but it was Arroyo who saved many of them, giving Houk a nearly unbeatable combination—Ford for the first seven or eight innings, and then Arroyo to finish up.

Between them, Ford and Arroyo won 40 games and lost only 9 that season. In the World Series, the Ford-Arroyo unit won three of the four games the Yanks needed to defeat the Cincinnati Reds for the world championship.

After his retirement from the Yankees, Whitey Ford took up harness racing. Owning several horses, Ford here drives Tarpot Birdie *to victory.*

In 1962, Ford dipped to 17 victories. But he shot up to 24 in 1963, his second and final 20-win campaign. Unlike the Stengel years—when he was "spotted" in the rotation for key games—Whitey pitched a league-leading 269 innings for Houk in 1963. He also set the American League pace for games started (37). But in the World Series his magic began to fade—he dropped two decisions to the Dodgers, who swept the Yankees in four straight games that year.

The Yankees' glory came to an end in 1964 with their final

pennant in a long string. They had captured the pennant in every year but two since 1949. The 1964 season was also the last really good one for Whitey Ford, who had been with New York for most of their great years.

Ford won 17 games in 1964 and dropped just six, but again he was unable to win a World Series game. The St. Louis Cardinals—led by another pitching star, Bob Gibson—took the championship in seven games. Ford's record slipped to 16–13 in 1965. Even more significant was his earned-run average, which

Whitey shows the ball he used to set a new World Series record of 33⅔ consecutive scoreless innings in 1961. The old record of 29⅔ innings was set by Babe Ruth when he pitched for the Boston Red Sox in 1916 and 1918.

soared from 2.13 in 1964 to 3.24 the following year.

In 1966, medical problems with his left shoulder and arm brought an end to a brilliant career. Whitey won just two games that season. He made an unsuccessful comeback attempt the next year, in which he won another two games. Then he decided to retire at the age of 38.

Ford remained with the Yankee organization after his retirement. He served as a minor league pitching instructor through the end of the 1967 season before moving up as the Yankees' pitching coach in 1968 and 1969. But

Whitey Ford later admitted that he did not feel comfortable in a regular coaching role. He retired for good after the 1969 season, serving only as an aide in spring training for the Yanks.

An Award Winner

Along with his World Series records, Ford also held the American League record for most consecutive games won as a rookie (nine in 1950). Whitey's lifetime earned-run average was 2.74. In 1961, he was the winner of the Cy Young Award. He was named Pitcher of the Year by *The Sporting News* in 1955, 1961, and 1963.

Along with Mickey Mantle, Billy Martin, and Hank Bauer, Ford had a reputation as a fun-lover off the field. But on the field his pitching marks stand as an example

of excellence that few hurlers of his era matched. For his cleverness and grace on the mound, Whitey Ford certainly earned his title— "the thinking-man's pitcher."

Further Study

BOOKS

Hickey, David and Kerry Keene. *The Proudest Yankees of All: From the Bronx to Cooperstown.* Lanham, MD: Taylor Trade Publishing, 2003.

Kisseloff, Jeff. *Who Is Baseball's Greatest Pitcher?* Chicago, IL: Cricket Books, 2003.

WEB SITES

Baseball Almanac. Online at www.baseball-almanac.com/players/ballplayer.shtml (October 2006)

"Whitey Ford," *National Baseball Hall of Fame and Museum.* Online at www.baseballhalloffame.org/hofers_and_honorees/hofer_bios/ford_whitey.htm (October 2006)

Career Highlights

All-time leader in World Series wins (10)

Led the American League in wins three times

Won the Cy Young Award and was named World Series MVP in 1961 with the New York Yankees

Compiled a career 236–106 record

Inducted into the Baseball Hall of Fame in 1974

♀Foreman, George

George Foreman (1949–   ), boxer, was born in Marshall, Texas, and brought up in a tough section of Houston. Two years after dropping out of school at 14, he entered the Job Corps where he learned bricklaying, carpentry, and electronics. He eventually earned the equivalent of a high school diploma. He was introduced to boxing by Charles R. "Doc" Broadus. Foreman fought his first amateur bout in 1967. He won the national Amateur Athletic Union (AAU) title in 1967, and the heavyweight gold medal in the 1968 Olympic games in Mexico City. After signing with professional manager Dick Sadler, Foreman fought and won 37 bouts from 1969 to 1972, taking all but three by knockouts. On January 22, 1973, Foreman faced heavyweight champion Joe Frazier. In less than two full rounds he knocked Frazier down

six times. The fight was stopped after 4 minutes and 35 seconds, giving George Foreman the heavyweight title of the world. Foreman lost the crown to Muhammad Ali in the "Rumble in the Jungle" fight in Zaire in 1974. Foreman retired from boxing in 1977, only to return 10 years later to recapture the heavyweight crown.

T he heavyweight championship is the most desired prize in boxing, and probably one of the most impressive titles of all sports. Winning the title is bound to affect a man's thinking in one way or another.

All too often, the man who wins the title considers it his personal property, something to be boasted about, carefully guarded, and used to make every possible dollar.

George Foreman appeared to have a different point of view. Mixed with Foreman's pride was a level-headed, common-sense approach, a measure of humanity, and even humility, which was rare among wearers of the heavyweight crown.

After Foreman defeated Joe Frazier in two rounds in one of the

Foreman gets some encouraging words from his trainer during the 1968 Olympics.

Foreman, George

(right) It's a battle of the eyes as champion Joe Frazier (left) and challenger George Foreman stare each other down at the weigh-in before their fight in 1973. Foreman upset Frazier and took the title.

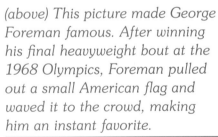

(above) This picture made George Foreman famous. After winning his final heavyweight bout at the 1968 Olympics, Foreman pulled out a small American flag and waved it to the crowd, making him an instant favorite.

ring's historic upsets, he made it clear that he was now calling the shots among the heavyweights. But at the same time he said, "The title is borrowed from the people and must be given back. I plan to take advantage of it while I can, and treat everybody good. And when it's time to give it up, I'll do so smiling."

And a few months later, passing up requests for television talk-show appearances, he flew instead to New York from his home in Hayward, California, to lend his support to the Special Olympics for mentally retarded young athletes.

"This is what I enjoy doing," he said in New York. "This is what life is all about. You look at these kids and what they can accomplish and it makes you proud of the American system."

Foreman was less excited about boxing. "I can't say I like fighting," he says. "I just like what I get from it."

The Early Years

George Foreman was born in Marshall, Texas, on January 10, 1949, the fifth of seven children of J.D. and Nancy Foreman. His father was a railroad construction worker.

George grew up in Houston's fifth ward, known as "The Bloody Fifth." A junior high school dropout at 14, he spent his days hanging around street corners. His companions were thieves and criminals, many of them involved in drugs.

"I had some minor juvenile scrapes, a few run-ins with the police, some street fights," he

Joe Frazier's knees buckle after Foreman lands a hard left. The smash brought Frazier to the canvas for the last time in the second round in the 1973 fight.

remembers. But he steered clear of serious trouble.

When he was 16, George heard of the Job Corps, where a young man could learn a trade, and even complete his education with the help of government funds. He decided to give it a try.

First he was sent to Grant's Pass, Oregon, where he learned bricklaying and carpentry. Then he moved on to Pleasanton, California, where he was taught electronics assembly work and earned the equivalent of a high school diploma. He also played football and attracted the attention of Charles R. "Doc" Broadus, the camp's sports director. Doc encouraged him to try boxing.

Doc Broadus was just the man to handle George Foreman. Although only 5-feet, 5-inches tall, Broadus had mastered judo and karate, as well as other arts of self-defense. He told George from the start, "You are bigger than me, but I can handle you, baby." It was clear that size was not important to him.

Doc Broadus knew that Foreman needed to be directed in a certain way. He made it his business to urge his fighter to keep on, even though the training was rough and the defeats hard to take.

Hard Going in the Ring

Foreman was not an instant success in the ring. The first time he put on the gloves, one of the camp's veterans beat him soundly and George did not return to the gym. Doc Broadus looked for him, and George came back, only to disappear once again before he was booked for a fight. But Doc kept after him, and on January 26, 1967, Foreman had his first formal amateur bout.

Foreman won the San Francisco Golden Gloves tournament in 1967 and went to the finals of

Foreman, George

Rocking the champion back on his feet, George Foreman (right) knocks Joe Frazier down again in the second round of their title fight in January of 1973. Challenger Foreman scored a TKO over champion Frazier to win the world heavyweight crown.

the nationals. Finishing his Job Corps training, he returned to Houston in July 1967, but could not find a job.

George Foreman became upset because no one would hire him, and he began to drift along the streets with nothing to do. Finally, he returned to California, where Doc got him a job at the Job Corps Center as a $465-a-month instructor. Foreman also resumed training under Broadus, who urged him to try for the Olympics.

"I didn't even know what the Olympics were then," Foreman

recalls with a laugh. But he worked hard and improved greatly.

Every day he ran a total of 10 miles—five in the morning and five at night. He also continued to coach the Job Corps team, and took boxing lessons from Broadus.

Although he lost a pair of decisions to Clay Hodges, the defending national American Athletic Union (AAU) champion, early in 1968, Foreman went on to capture that title and become a member of the U.S. Olympic team.

At the Olympics

At the Olympics in Mexico City, the young boxer, still a little crude and unpolished, beat boxers from Poland, Romania, Italy, and Russia to win the Olympic heavyweight gold medal. When the crowd cheered his victory, George took a tiny U.S. flag from the pocket of his ring robe and waved it. This proud, spur-of-the-moment gesture made him a worldwide celebrity overnight.

Now it was clear to him that he would try to make a career as a professional fighter. He was offered lots of money to sign with many different managers, but he turned all these offers down. After

(right) Swamped by fans, Foreman heads for the dressing room after soundly defeating Joe Frazier for the world heavyweight title.

eight months of thinking it over, he finally signed with Dick Sadler, a veteran boxing man best known for having trained Archie Moore and Sonny Liston toward the end of their careers.

"All I can offer you is a lifetime of mistakes," said Sadler. "And lot of hard work."

Sadler knew Foreman's good points, but he also understood his shortcomings. George was big (6 feet, 3 inches, 220 pounds) and strong, and a hard puncher, but

It's homecoming as Foreman returns to E.O. Smith Junior High School, where he attended as a youth. The young fans are excited to see the new champion.

"God blesses me with the ability to take away your title. Don't worry. It won't go to waste. I'll make good use of it."
—George Foreman, predicting he would defeat champion Joe Frazier

Foreman, George

As the founder of the Job Corps, President Lyndon Johnson had a big effect on the life of George Foreman. Foreman got his start in the Corps and was the first graduate to become famous in sports. Here Foreman presents the president a plaque honoring him for starting the Corps, shortly after Foreman won the 1968 heavyweight boxing Olympic gold medal. Ironically, President Johnson passed away the very same night that Foreman won the world heavyweight title, January 22, 1973.

he knew little about defense or balance, two important parts of good boxing. Sadler set out to teach him first in the gym, then in actual fights.

Foreman made his pro debut on June 23, 1969, scoring a three-round knockout over an unknown fighter named Don Waldhelm. In the next three-and-a-half years he had 36 more bouts, all over the country. He won all but three by knockouts. But few of his opponents were much better known than Waldhelm. Those who were—such as Gregorio Peralta, George Chuvalo, and Roberto Davila—had seen better days.

The newspapers demanded that Foreman face tougher op-position, but Sadler stuck to his program.

"He's still learning," he insisted. "My job is to see that he is prepared when the time comes."

The New Champion

The big chance arrived on January 22, 1973, at Kingston, Jamaica. Hardly anyone thought that Foreman's 37–0 record against unknowns could have prepared him to stand up against Joe Frazier, who was looking forward to signing for a rematch with Muhammad Ali—after he had defeated George in Jamaica.

But the underdog Foreman toyed with Frazier, dropping him three times in the first round and three times more in the second. When the end came after only 4 minutes and 35 seconds of one-sided action, Frazier was dizzy and bleeding. The 36,000 fans cheered a new champion, a man of great power, yet a kind man who had actually asked the referee to stop the match so he would not have to continue punishing his opponent.

"God blesses me with the ability to take away your title," George Foreman had told Frazier several months before the fight. "Don't worry. It won't go to waste. I'll make good use of it."

Three champs laugh it up. George Foreman (left) is all smiles after his defeat of Joe Frazier that gave him the heavyweight title in 1973. Also enjoying his victory are former heavyweight champion Joe Louis (middle) and former light-heavyweight titleholder, Archie Moore.

In 1974, Foreman was taunted and eventually beaten himself by the athletic and mobile Muhammad Ali. Foreman continued to fight until he was beaten in 1977 by Jimmy Young, at which time he decided to hang up his gloves and preach the Gospel as a minister.

After 10 years in the pulpit, Foreman returned to the ring. His comeback included losses to

Career Highlights

Won the National AAU championship in 1967

Olympic heavyweight champ at 1968 Mexico City Games

Won the world heavyweight championship in 1973, knocking out Joe Frazier

Recaptured the heavyweight title on November 5, 1994, at age 45 with a 10-round KO of WBA/IBF champ Michael Moorer, becoming the oldest man to win the heavyweight crown

Named 1994 Associated Press Male Athlete of Year, 20 years after losing his earlier title to Muhammad Ali

Evander Holyfield and Tommy Morrison and a win over Gerry Cooney. Foreman's comeback culminated in a 10th round KO (knockout) of champ Michael Moorer in Las Vegas, Nevada, on November 5, 1994. George Foreman had regained the heavyweight championship (combined World Boxing Association/International Boxing Federation) of the world, 20 years after he had lost it.

The WBA later stripped Foreman of its designation as champion, since he had not fought the top contender, Tony Tucker. On June 29, 1995, the IBF followed suit, stripping Foreman of the championship.

In the late 1990s, Foreman became best known as a product promoter for cooking equipment. He also appeared as a boxing analyst for HBO broadcasts of professional bouts.

Further Study

BOOKS

Hunter, Shaun. *Great African Americans in the Olympics.* New York: Crab Tree, 1997.

Knapp, Ron. *Top 10 Heavyweight Boxers.* Springfield, NJ: Enslow, 1997.

McCoyd, Ed. *To Live and Dream: The Incredible Story of George Foreman.* New York: New Street, 1997.

WEB SITES

"George Foreman," *International Boxing Hall of Fame.* Online at www.ibhof.com/foreman.htm (October 2006)

⏱ Fosbury, Dick

Dick Fosbury (1947–   ), high jumper, was born in Portland, Oregon. In high school, he used the common straddle-roll style of high jumping with no success. He then thought of trying to clear the bar backward and, as a result, improved his marks. He attended Oregon State University. There, his coach, Berny Wagner, told him to go back to the traditional way of high jumping. Fosbury did, but only for a year. He went back to jumping backward as a sophomore and by 1968 had cleared 7 feet. In the same year, he won the National Collegiate Athletic Association (NCAA) indoor title with his best jump yet—7 feet, 1½ inches. He also won the outdoor NCAA championship with a jump of 7 feet, 2¼ inches. Fosbury then won the gold medal at the 1968 Olympic Games in Mexico City with a jump of 7 feet,

4½ inches. His unique and innovative style was dubbed the "Fosbury Flop." By the 1972 Olympic Games in Munich, West Germany, many of the world's best high jumpers were flopping backward. Later, Dick Fosbury competed professionally in the International Track Association.

The man who turned the high-jumping event upside down was Dick Fosbury, originator of the "Fosbury Flop."

Such major changes as Fosbury's in the basics of track-and-field events are rare. Even the most creative athletes and coaches work to refine skills that are already standard rather than develop new approaches. But working with what he felt was a simpler method, Dick Fosbury created a revolutionary new technique for high jumping. The idea caught on and was spread across the world through news stories and television coverage of Fosbury's gold medal performance in the 1968 Olympics in Mexico City.

Richard D. Fosbury was born March 6, 1947, in Portland,

Dick just gets over the bar with his "Fosbury Flop."

Fosbury, Dick

Oregon. As a high school athlete, he tried the standard straddle-roll of high jumping with little success. It was a struggle for him to leap 5 feet, 4 inches. Then the idea of jumping backward came to him. In his first meet using the new style, Dick Fosbury raised his best mark from 5 feet, 4 inches to 5 feet, 10 inches—6 full inches.

But success did not come without a price. "None of our opponents in high school could afford foam-rubber landing pits," Fosbury commented later. "So I would have to jump into sawdust pits. Landing on my back so much compressed two vertebrae in my spine." Despite the physical pain, Fosbury continued to work on his new technique.

In 1965, he entered Oregon State University in Corvallis. The new freshman showed his odd jumping style to coach Berny Wagner. "Go back to the old style," the coach said. During his first college season, Dick Fosbury obeyed his coach. He went back to planting his left foot on the ground and kicking his right leg up and over the bar, rolling over in a straddle position.

But Fosbury was unhappy with his return to the normal style. "The roll is so complicated," he

"I was told over and over again that I would never be successful, that I was not going to be competitive and the technique was simply not going to work. All I could do was shrug and say, 'We'll just have to see.'"
—Dick Fosbury, on his revolutionary high-jumping technique

said. "I just never had the coordination for jumping that way." He went on, "There are so many things to think about when jumping with the roll."

As his sophomore year began, Fosbury went back to his style of jumping backward. He would run up to the bar, plant his right foot, and thrust upward with his left knee, as if trying to hit his chin. He then arched his back over the bar, throwing his feet high into the air, and landed on his neck and shoulders in the pit. He labored to gain strength and to free himself of habits picked up while using the straddle-roll the year before.

The Fosbury Flop

At the start of the 1968 track season, Dick Fosbury was ready. Several indoor track directors invited the 6-foot, 4-inch, 184-pound Oregon State junior to their meets. After several competitions, Fosbury successfully cleared 7 feet. The blond jumper soon became a favorite at meets, and his attention-getting style was dubbed the "Fosbury Flop."

During the rest of the indoor track season, Dick Fosbury "flopped" successfully over 7 feet four times. The last of those 7-footers earned him the National Collegiate Athletic Association

(NCAA) indoor title as he reached a personal best of 7 feet, 1½ inches.

Then, during the outdoor season, Fosbury showed his true competitiveness. He was charged with the urge to be the best—no second place for him. Winning was all-important and his goals stretched higher and higher.

After the spring season of dual meets, early summer brought the championship events. Dick Fosbury won the Pacific-8 meet in Berkeley, California, with his first outdoor 7-foot jump. Four weeks later at the NCAA championships, Fosbury faced a tough field of seven other high jumpers who had cleared the 7-foot level. For two days the jumpers soared over the bar as it slowly inched upward. Not missing a single jump, Fosbury "flopped" successfully on his first try at each new height. Finally, at 7 feet, 2¼ inches, Fosbury won. Fans, rivals, and experts all began to take the 21-year-old's strange methods seriously.

Olympic Tryouts

The time for the choice of an Olympic team for the Olympic Games to be held in Mexico City came at the end of June. And although Fosbury had proved himself at the Pacific-8 and NCAA

Fosbury, Dick

meets, many held doubts that the "Fosbury Flop" would stand up in the high-pressure Olympic competition. At the semifinal U.S. Olympic trials in Los Angeles on June 30, Fosbury proved his "flop" again. Before jumping, he went through a ritual of rocking back and forth while clenching his fists. Then, flying down the runway with long strides, he pushed upward, arched his back, and flipped his legs over the bar at 7 feet—and won first place.

Later, at the final U.S. Olympic trials held at South Lake Tahoe on the California-Nevada border, Fosbury cleared 7 feet, and 7 feet, 1 inch with his first attempts. But

Career Highlights

Innovator of the "Fosbury Flop," a revolutionary backward high-jumping technique

Captured the 1968 NCAA indoor high-jump title by clearing 7 feet, 1½ inches

Added the 1968 NCAA outdoor championship with a height of 7 feet, 2¼ inches

Won a gold medal at the 1968 Summer Olympics

at 7 feet, 2 inches he failed in his first attempt, and then failed again. Yet he had jumped that height before, and he knew he could do it again. On his third and last try, he cleared the bar easily. He went on to jump 7 feet, 3 inches on his first attempt. Fosbury set a personal record—and earned a berth on the Olympic team.

The altitude at the Lake Tahoe training area was similar to Mexico City's 7500 feet above sea level. By the time the Olympic Games came in October, Fosbury was ready. In the qualifying rounds on October 19, Dick Fosbury faced 14 other jumpers who had cleared 7 feet. But Fosbury was prepared for the pressure. He soared over every height on the first try in the qualifying rounds.

The next day's competition in the finals was a long one. Thirteen jumpers were entered. The contest began in midafternoon, and Fosbury smoothly cleared the opening height of 6 feet, 8 inches. His offbeat style gained wide notice each time he approached the bar. The level was upped to 6 feet, 10¼ inches and then 7 feet, ¼

inch. Fosbury topped both heights. Then the Russian Gavrilov passed his turn, adding to the tension in the air.

Each time a jumper neared the bar, the 80,000 spectators grew hushed. All three remaining contestants cleared the 7-foot, 2⅝-inch mark easily. As the bar went up to the 7-foot, 3⅜-inch point, Fosbury concentrated harder than ever before. He then ran to the bar and soared over on his first leap. A huge smile lit his face as he jumped up from the pit. The Russian Gavrilov, appearing tired, missed on all three of his jumps. Only Edward Carruthers and Fosbury were now left.

After three hours of grueling competition, Fosbury's willpower and confidence still held strong. The bar was set at 7 feet, 4¼

Landing on his head after clearing the bar at 7 feet, 2 inches, Dick Fosbury later won this meet with a leap of 7 feet, 4 inches.

inches, more than an inch above his best pre-Olympic jump. The young Oregon jumper stood with his eyes shut, rocking to and fro. He clenched his fists again, raced toward the bar—and missed. At his second try, he missed once more. When later asked what he thought of just before leaping, Fosbury recalled, "I just thought about floating over the bar." He knew he could do it.

A Gold Medal

As the young jumper set himself for his final jump, the marathon runners were winding their way back into the stadium. Fosbury concentrated on the high bar, gathered his strength, and ran toward the barrier. With a tremendous surge, he hurled his body upward, arched his back—and cleared the mark. A marathon runner, Ken Moore of Oregon, danced a jig on the track as Fosbury bounced back out of the pit with his hands stretched high. The gold medal was Fosbury's.

The fans in the stadium burst out in a roar of joy, cheering the grinning jumper. "I'm as tired as I've ever been," the new hero admitted moments after.

The "Fosbury Flop" continued to grow in popularity. Many of the world's great high jumpers turned to the backward method by the time the 1972 Olympic Games were held in Munich, West Germany.

The originator of the jump went on competing in his final year at Oregon State. Then in 1973, Dick Fosbury joined other track-and-field stars as a member of Mike O'Hara's newly formed professional league, the International Track Association. The "Flop" had taken its place with older standard methods of high jumping.

Further Study

WEB SITES

"Richard Douglas Fosbury," *International Olympic Committee.* Online at www.olympic.org/uk/athletes/profiles/bio_uk.asp?PAR_I_ID=18061 (October 2006)

⬤Four Horsemen

The Four Horsemen, Notre Dame football players, formed probably the most famous college backfield of all time. They consisted of quarterback Harry Stuhldreher (STOOL-drair) (1901–65), who was born in Massillon, Ohio; left halfback Jim Crowley (1902–86), born in Green Bay, Wisconsin; right halfback Don Miller (1902–79), born in Defiance, Ohio; and fullback Elmer Layden (1903–73), born in Davenport, Iowa. Playing together in the same backfield during the 1923 and 1924 seasons, the Fighting Irish lost only one game. Their great play inspired Grantland Rice to use their nickname in one of the most famous newspaper sports stories of all time. In their final college contest, the Four Horsemen led Notre Dame to a victory over Stanford University in the 1925 Rose Bowl. Stuhldreher, Crowley, and Layden were chosen as All-Americans in 1924. All of them went on to pursue coaching careers following very short careers in professional football. They were all elected to the National Football Foundation College Football Hall of Fame.

As a backfield unit, the Four Horsemen of Notre Dame rode to football fame from 1922 to the 1925 Rose Bowl. Together, they formed a unique combination of speed and perfect timing. It is even more surprising that the heaviest of the Horsemen was left halfback Jim Crowley at 164 pounds. Harry Stuhldreher, at quarterback, weighed 151; right halfback Don Miller, 160; and fullback Elmer Layden, 162.

In the Bible, the Four Horsemen of the Apocalypse are supposed to represent famine, pestilence, destruction, and death that are to come at the end of the world. George Strickler, the Notre Dame publicity man, had just been to the theater to see Rudolph Valentino in a movie about these Biblical "Four Horsemen." When he saw the Notre Dame backfield in action at their 1924 game against Army at New York's Polo Grounds, he got the idea for naming the four star players "The Four Horsemen."

Sportswriter Grantland Rice picked up the name and it stuck. Rice wrote in his story on the game:

"Outlined against a blue-gray October sky, The Four Horsemen rode again. In dramatic lore, they are known as famine, pestilence, destruction, and death. These are only aliases. Their real names are Stuhldreher, Miller, Crowley, and Layden. They formed the crest of the South Bend cyclone before which another fighting Army team was swept over the precipice at the Polo Grounds this afternoon as 55,000 spectators peered down upon the bewildering panorama spread out upon the green plain below."

The next Monday afternoon, back in South Bend, Indiana, Strickler brought four horses and a photographer to the Notre Dame football practice field. He stopped practice to photograph the fleet backs on the four horses. It proved to be one of the most famous sports photos ever taken.

To Knute Rockne, coach of the Notre Dame Fighting Irish, the formation of the famous backfield was an accident of history. Rockne had not been impressed with any of the four when he watched them play as freshmen. "Not so hot,"

Rockne thought, "especially when the entire four were smeared by a clumsy but willing scrub tackle who weighed about as much as the entire quartet and pounded through like an ice wagon to block a kick."

Sleepy Jim Crowley

Jim Crowley was born September 10, 1902, in Green Bay, Wisconsin. He had been coached in high school by Curly Lambeau. Lambeau had played under Rockne, and he later organized and coached the pro Green Bay Packers.

The Four Horsemen pose on horseback during a 1924 Notre Dame practice.

Crowley was the only one of the famous four who had a nickname. Once when Coach Rockne was explaining a play at practice, he noticed that Crowley's head was nodding and his eyes were staring blankly. Rockne asked Crowley if he got enough sleep at night. Crowley replied that he got enough sleep at night, but that he had trouble getting enough sleep in the afternoons—during football. After that, he was called "Sleepy

Four Horsemen

Jim Crowley, with his dark heavy eyes and expressionless face, earned the nickname "Sleepy."

the freshman. "He could run the 100-yard dash in under 10 seconds. But speed and some kicking ability seemed to be all his football wares."

During his first year in college, Layden almost left school because he was homesick. He was in the train station asking about trains back to Iowa when two older Notre Dame football players saw him. The next thing Layden knew, he was in Knute Rockne's office. Layden was telling Rockne how he thought he was too small at 150 pounds to play football. Suddenly, Rockne said, "Layden, what's this I hear about your going home?"

"Well," said Layden, "I've thought about it." Then, said Rockne, "If you go home, you'll have one distinction! You'll be the first freshman Notre Dame ever lost because of homesickness!" Layden was cured of his homesickness. Layden died June 30, 1973.

Miller Has Instinct

Don Miller was born March 29, 1902, in Defiance, Ohio. He and his brother, Gerry, who entered Notre Dame at the same time, fol-

Jim." Crowley died January 15, 1986.

Layden Has the Speed

Elmer Layden was born May 4, 1903, in Davenport, Iowa. Layden came to Notre Dame as a bas- ketball prospect. His high school football coach, Walter Halas, came to Notre Dame in 1921 to be Rockne's assistant and scout. Elmer Layden played every sport with almost equal ease. "Layden had speed," said Rockne observing

lowed their football-playing brothers Red, Walter, and Roy to Notre Dame. Gerry played first string as a freshman, but by the middle of his sophomore year, he was replaced by Don. Don surprised Rockne with his speed and daring. Miller soon was a full-fledged regular at right halfback. He had football instinct. Miller died July 28, 1979.

Stuhldreher Has the Most Promise

Harry Stuhldreher was born October 14, 1901, in Massillon, Ohio. When he was in high school, Harry worked after school delivering groceries with a horse and wagon for his father's store. He wanted to play football, but his job took too much time. He began putting on regular clothes over his football uniform and racing the horse and wagon through the streets to get his deliveries finished so he could practice football. After a few weeks, his father noticed that the poor horse came home hot and lathered and was losing weight. To save the horse, Harry's father let his son take time off from his deliveries to play football. Princeton tried to recruit Stuhldreher, but he decided to go to Notre Dame, where his brother Walter was attending college.

Knute Rockne remembered Stuhldreher's play as a freshman. "Stuhldreher, of the lot, had the most promise. He sounded like a leader on the field. He was a good and fearless blocker, and as he gained football knowledge, he showed signs of smartness in emergencies." Stuhldreher died January 26, 1965.

In 1922, the sophomore year for the Four Horsemen, Stuhldreher was promoted to alternate quarterback. Likewise, Layden got his chance at fullback when All-America candidate Paul Castner suffered a broken hip. That gave Rockne a knife-like

fullback (Layden), a speedy right half (Crowley), a snake-hipped left half (Miller)—all directed by Stuhldreher, a smart and natural leader. The famous line, behind which the Four Horsemen played, was called "the Seven Mules" and was led by team captain Adam Walsh.

The First Group Outing

They played together for the first time against Carnegie Institute of Technology at Pittsburgh in 1922, and for 21 games after that. They had timing, alertness, and speed, and they played from 30 to 40 minutes every game. Since Stuhldreher and Crowley were slower

Four Horsemen

plowed up the ground to make it softer. The soft field really put the brakes on the light Notre Dame backfield.

By the time of the all-important 1924 Nebraska game—in the senior year of the Four Horsemen—Miller had become an exceptional broken-field runner. Layden was both a fine runner and punter, as well as a talented pass-defender. Crowley was a fearless blocker, and on defense he would tackle anybody.

In that 1924 Nebraska game, Rockne started out with his second team. They fumbled on their

Career Highlights

Led Notre Dame to a 10–0 record and national championship following the 1925 Rose Bowl victory over Stanford

Lost only one game in a two-year span

Three of the four were chosen as All-Americans in 1924

All were elected to the National Football Foundation Hall of Fame—Layden in 1951, Stuhldreher in 1958, Crowley in 1966, and Miller in 1970

than Layden and Miller, Rockne gave them lighter shoes, pads, and socks. Rockne also had Stuhldreher pass mostly to the other backs, instead of to the ends.

The next season, as juniors, the Horsemen rolled up 275 points to their opponents' 37. The only game they lost was against the University of Nebraska Cornhuskers. Nebraska had one of the heaviest teams in the country, and they pushed the lightweight Notre Dame team all over the field. The Nebraska school had been unable to grow grass on their field, so they

three-yard line, giving Nebraska an easy touchdown. The Horsemen evened up the score in the second period with Stuhldreher's passing. From then on, Notre Dame ran away with the game. Crowley raced 80 yards with a pass to score. Stuhldreher shot two more touchdown passes to Miller, and then Layden plunged for the final score in the 34–6 conquest. Notre Dame finished off the season unbeaten in all 10 games. They were Rose Bowl bound.

Rockne opened the Rose Bowl game against Stanford University with his second team, the "shock troops." The Stanford Indians grabbed a 3–0 lead. Led by Ernie Nevers, they outgained the Irish. But the speed and timing of the Four Horsemen proved too much for Stanford. Layden intercepted a Stanford pass and streaked 78 yards to score, giving Notre Dame a 13–3 lead at halftime. Layden picked off another Stanford pass in the final period and ran 70 yards to his third touchdown to lift the final score to 27–10.

Crowley, Layden, and Stuhldreher were named All-American, and all four Horsemen were named to the National Football Foundation College Football Hall of Fame. All four played for a short time in pro leagues.

Coaching College Ball

The talents that made the Horsemen great football players also made them fine coaches. All of them served as college coaches. Layden returned to Notre Dame as head coach in 1934, where he had a record of 47–13–1. Many people feel that he was the best coach Notre Dame ever had. In 1940, Layden became commissioner of pro football and served until 1946.

With Rockne at the reins, the Four Horsemen compiled a 25–2–1 record and outscored foes, 755–108, in their three seasons.

No other college team has been as publicized or won such national and lasting fame as the 1924 Four Horsemen squad. They conquered every rival team and beat Stanford in the Rose Bowl on New Year's Day, 1925.

Further Study

"Traditions: The Four Horsemen," *University of Notre Dame.* Online at und.ocsn.com/trads/horse.html (October 2006)

"The Four Horsemen Ride Again, on a Stamp" *Notre Dame Magazine.* Online at www.nd.edu/~ndmag/dom3su98. html (October 2006)

⚾ Foxx, Jimmie

Jimmie Foxx (1907–1967), baseball player, was born in Sudlersville, Maryland. In his youth Foxx wanted to be a track star, but he ended up playing on his high school baseball team. Foxx broke into professional baseball as a catcher in 1924. He joined the Philadelphia Athletics in 1925, but was used sparingly until he was switched to first base in 1928. In the next 13 consecutive years, Foxx had over 100 runs batted in (RBIs). He set a record by hitting over 30 home runs for 12 straight seasons

(1929–40). In 1932 he hit 58 homers. He led the Athletics to the 1929 and 1930 world championships and won the Most Valuable Player (MVP) award three times. He ended his career with 534 home runs and a batting average of .325. He was elected to the Baseball Hall of Fame in 1951.

Jimmie Foxx had much in common with Babe Ruth as a ballplayer—with one notable exception.

Foxx was baseball's most feared right-handed hitter during the 1930s and rivaled Ruth both as a slugger and fun-lover. But Ruth received a salary of $80,000 during his best year, while Foxx never made more than $32,000 in any one season. Most of the time he was paid far less.

His low pay during most of his career, along with overly generous acts and poor business moves,

marked Foxx's later years. "I guess I was born to be broke," he noted near the end of his life. He was almost penniless when he died.

Yet Foxx's slugging feats remain legends. He played for nearly 20 years in the majors, most of them with the Philadelphia Athletics and the Boston Red Sox. He compiled a lifetime batting average of .325, blasted 534 home runs, and three times was named Most Valuable Player (MVP) in the American League.

A member of the Hall of Fame, Jimmie Foxx was famous

for his long home runs. Many of these have never been equaled. According to baseball historian Ed Walton, "In virtually every AL park, there was a story to tell about a mighty Foxx homer. In Chicago, he hit a ball over the double-decked stands at Comiskey Park, clearing 34th Street. His gigantic clout in Cleveland won the 1935 All-Star Game. In Yankee Stadium, his blast high into the left field upper deck had enough power to break a seat. In St. Louis, his ninth inning blast in Game Five of the 1930 Series just about clinched it for the A's. In Detroit, he hit one

of the longest balls ever, way up into the left field bleachers." He hit 30 or more homers for 12 straight seasons and drove in at least 100 runs for 13 years in a row between 1929 and 1941.

The Early Years

Born in Sudlersville, Maryland, on October 22, 1907, James Emory Foxx was the son of Sarr Dell Foxx, a farmer. At 10, Jimmie ran away from home to enlist in the Army as a drummer boy. Rejected by the Army, he turned his attention to sports. His first love was track, even though he was short and stocky. He grew up wanting to be the fastest sprinter in the country.

Jimmie Foxx first showed his baseball skills as a member of the Sudlersville High School team. In high school he played several positions. This varied experience later helped his big-league career.

While still a high school student, Jimmie caught the eye of Frank "Home Run" Baker, a former big-league star. Baker was then managing Easton in the Class D Maryland Eastern Shore League. Baker was impressed with Foxx's power and asked him to come for a tryout.

Jimmie Foxx, then only 16, got permission from his father to quit school after promising to return in the fall. He went to Easton, hoping to play third base or pitch. But Baker was short of catchers, and he asked Foxx to work behind the plate.

Foxx was a standout right from the start, batting .296 in 76 games. Both the New York Yankees and the Philadelphia Athletics spoke to Frank Baker about the youngster. Baker, who had played with both teams, advised Jimmie to go with Philadelphia and play under Connie Mack.

Mack was not eager at first to take Foxx. He already had two catchers in young Mickey

Foxx, Jimmie

Philadelphia Athletics owner Connie Mack gives encouragement to his ace, Jimmie Foxx.

In his first year as a regular, Foxx became the terror of the league. Short and muscular, he was built like a tank. Deep in the batter's box with a wide stance, he took a full stride into the ball. His powerful arm muscles would visibly flex as his bat met the ball with a thunderous crack. Because of his strength and his powerful, long hits, sportswriters dubbed him "The Maryland Strongboy." He batted .354, drove in 117 runs, and hit 33 homers, leading the A's to their first pennant in 15 years.

Cochrane and veteran Cy Perkins, and he felt he did not need another one. But Baker persisted.

"Please take him," Baker said. "He can hit with more power than any hitter I've seen, including Ruth. You'll find a place for him somewhere."

Foxx joined the Athletics in 1924. He rode the bench the first year. In 1925 he went to bat nine times and got six hits, but spent most of the season at Providence.

In 1926 he was back with the A's, but he spent most of the season as a backup catcher to Cochrane. This time he got into

only 26 games, mostly as a pinch-hitter, and batted .313.

A Chance to Play

The following year the A's began to use him more behind the plate, often against left-handed pitchers. Foxx played in 61 games, batted .323, and hit his first three big-league homers. Connie Mack began trying Foxx at different positions in 1928 and used him in 118 games. Foxx responded with a .328 batting average and 13 homers. The following spring he had become the team's regular first baseman.

By 1932 he had become one of the game's true superstars. Fans began calling him "Double X" and "The Beast" because of his many home runs. In 1932, the best season of his career, he belted 58 homers, batted .364, and drove in 169 runs. He received the first of his three MVP awards.

The next year he was again chosen MVP. He also captured the Triple Crown—an honor earned by the player having the most home runs in the league during a single year, the most runs batted in (RBIs), and the highest batting average.

But times were tough. The Great Depression had reached its peak in the early 1930s, and dollars were scarce. To save the franchise, Connie Mack was forced to unload his team of superstars, one at a time. After 10 years with Philadelphia, Foxx was traded to the Boston Red Sox in December 1935.

Losing Off the Diamond

With the Red Sox, Foxx finally began to earn money worthy of his talents. But while his stock increased on the field, his off-the-field investments were flops. He had lost heavily in the stock market crash of 1929. Alimony payments to his first wife cut deep into his savings.

But perhaps his greatest weakness was his generosity. Foxx was forever giving money to friends in need, buying a round for the boys, or spending heavily on a night on the town. Foxx's battle with the bottle helped to break his health and bring an early end to his career.

The Red Sox released him on waivers to the Chicago Cubs in 1942. He wound up his career with the Philadelphia Phillies in 1945—batting .268 at the age of 37 and being used as a part-time pitcher.

Had Foxx been able to play one more year he would have qualified for the players' pension fund. This fund was set up to include all players on big-league teams after September 1946.

After his retirement as a player, Foxx did some managing in the minor leagues. Although he had earned $270,000 playing baseball, he hit on hard times in the late 1950s. By 1958 he was penniless.

As soon as his poverty became known, job offers began pouring in from many of his friends. He took a job with the Red Sox as a coach for their Minneapolis farm team in the American Association.

In 1967, while visiting his brother's home, Jimmie Foxx choked at dinner and died.

In his later years, when ballplayers were receiving more in bonus money than he was paid during his entire career, Jimmie Foxx would sadly say, "Baseball was mighty good to me, but I was born ten years too soon."

Career Highlights

Hit over 30 home runs for 12 straight seasons (1929–40)

Led American League in home runs four times and batting twice

Won the Triple Crown in 1933, smacking 48 home runs with 168 RBIs and a .356 average

Three-time MVP (1932, 1933, 1938) with Philadelphia and Boston

Compiled 534 career home runs and a career average of .325

Inducted into the Baseball Hall of Fame in 1951

⌾ Foyt, A.J.

A.J. (Anthony Joseph, Jr.) Foyt (1935–   ), racecar driver, was born in Houston, Texas. When he was 3 years old, his father, a garage owner and midget-car racer, built a gas-powered miniature racer for him. At 11, A.J. was racing his father's midgets. Shortly after making his professional racing debut at Houston's Playland Park, he became a well-known midget car and stock car racer. Foyt later went on to become perhaps the greatest all-round driver in history. He won the United States Auto Club (USAC) driving championship seven times. A.J. Foyt was the first to win the Indianapolis 500 four times—1961,

1964, 1967, and 1977. He had more victories in Indy-Car competition (67) than any other driver. He won all three major endurance races in the world. He was named Driver of the Year in 1975, and tied with Mario Andretti in the Associated Press balloting for Driver of the Century, announced in December 1999.

The only driver in history to win the Indianapolis 500, the Daytona 500, and the 24 Hours of Le Mans is A.J. Foyt.

With only 15 laps left in the 1977 Indianapolis 500, three-time winner A.J. Foyt was in second place behind Gordon Johncock. Ten long years had passed since Foyt had taken the race, and it looked like he had fallen short again. Suddenly, Johncock's engine failed. As Gordon's crippled car slid onto the infield grass, Foyt's eight-cylinder, orange-colored Coyote sped by to take the checkered flag. A.J. Foyt had won the Indy for a record fourth time.

Expertise and daring made Foyt a great driver. That fourth Indianapolis win was his 58th win overall on the National Championship Trail circuit, more than any other driver. He also won in other types of competition, ranging from sports cars in Europe to sprint and stock cars in the United States. The seven-time United States Auto Club (USAC) national champion was one of the last of a breed who were both mechanics and drivers.

A.J. Foyt was perhaps the greatest driver in auto-racing history. Fellow driver Junior Johnson said, "Foyt could drive anything, anywhere, anytime."

The Early Years

The son of a mechanic and driver, Anthony Joseph Foyt, Jr., was born in Houston, Texas, on January 16, 1935. When he was 3, his father built him a small electric car shaped like a racer. When he

A.J. roars past the crowd at the Indianapolis Speedway.

was 5, his father built him a junior gasoline-powered car. It had a four-speed gearbox, and it would go 55 miles per hour. Young A.J. drove it between races at the tracks where his father competed. He once won a challenge race with the car at the Houston Speed Bowl.

One day his parents took one of their midget racers to an out-of-town track to race, leaving their backup car and young A.J. at home. They returned home to find the backyard torn up, and grass thrown against the house and fence. In the garage sat the backup car, scorched and dirty. Their son

was in bed. A.J. had been skidding the car around the yard, dirt-track style, but had quit after the car caught fire.

Foyt left Lamar High School in Houston in the 11th grade so he could go into racing full-time. He raced on dirt tracks in midgets, sprint cars, and stock cars. Soon, A.J. Foyt would become the best-known driver in Texas.

When he was 20, A.J. married Lucy Zarr, and they began going to the Indianapolis 500 as spectators. They even took their

infant son, A.J. III, soon after he was born.

Foyt was getting acquainted with some of the drivers of Championship cars, along with building a name as a dirt-track driver.

Qualifying for the Indy 500

In 1958, he took the Indianapolis Speedway's driver test. He did well enough to be asked to qualify a car for the race. He was the 12th-fastest qualifier, which put him in the fourth row in the starting lineup.

43

> *"I've never, ever, seen Foyt do anything foolish out on a racetrack. Never."*
>
> —Mario Andretti, on A.J. Foyt's driving precision

Foyt, A.J.

The 1958 race was a scary one. Fourteen cars piled up at the start, killing one driver and putting eight cars out of action. Later in the race, A.J. hit an oil slick and skidded backward for 958 feet. But for the most part, he threaded his way through the danger spots and went on to finish the 200-lap race, coming in 16th. He had survived his baptism of fire, and he would be back for more.

Foyt drove in 10 Championship races in 1958 and finished well ahead of many more experienced drivers. He also went on the Midwest sprint circuit and finished second to the great Eddie Sachs.

A.J. got into the good money at Indianapolis in 1959 when he ran fifth for most of the race, then settled back in 10th. For the year, he collected $60,000 in prizes, winning 10 USAC-sanctioned races.

The next year, Foyt hit it big and got into the running for the USAC national championship, which is based on points given for finishes in individual races during the year. A.J. was a few points ahead of Rodger Ward going into the final race at Phoenix, Arizona.

Four-time Indy winner A.J. Foyt waits as his crew adds fuel and changes tires during a pit stop.

Foyt set out to win the race as the best strategy to keep his lead over Ward. A.J. drove hard, forcing Ward to blow his engine. After that happened, Foyt could have relaxed, come in fifth, and still won the championship.

But race drivers of Foyt's caliber are never satisfied with anything less than first. A.J. opened up his lead to two full laps over the second-place car and easily won the race and the championship.

In this three-picture sequence,
A.J. Foyt spins out during
the 1965 Atlanta 250, jumps
from his car, and collapses
in the grass.

Number One

In four years' time, Foyt had gone from being ranked 109 in the USAC ratings to number one. That gave him the exclusive right to put the number "1" on his car. Foyt did not change his personality after he got to the top. He still mixed his moments of being generous, easygoing, and a practical joker with the moments when he was silent and remote.

In 1961, Foyt and Eddie Sachs got into one of the most exciting duels in the 45 runnings of the Indianapolis 500. They drove the whole last half of the race just a few feet apart, with first one, then the other, in the lead.

Finally, Foyt was able to move ahead by one second, then two. On the 185th lap of the 200-lap race, Foyt was four seconds ahead. His pit crew had not been able to fill his tank full on his last fuel stop, so Foyt now had to pit again. Sachs shot into the lead, and it looked as if Sachs would be a sure winner.

Foyt charged back onto the track and was running almost half a lap behind Sachs. Only 12 cars were left in the race. Foyt began to push his car to record speeds. Suddenly, with three laps to go, Sachs slowed down. The strain of

the high-speed duel with Foyt had ruined Eddie's right rear tire. He pitted for a tire change, but by the time he got back on the track, Foyt had clinched his first Indy title.

It was one of 19 USAC triumphs for A.J. that year. He had established himself as a man to beat, whether he was at Indianapolis or on a dirt track.

Foyt won the Indianapolis 500 again in 1964 and 1967. The 1964 victory marked the last time that a front-engine car won the race.

After the rear-engine machines began to dominate, Foyt designed and built his own car—a Ford-powered Coyote—and drove it to victory in 1967.

Foyt, A.J.

The 1967 victory was perhaps the toughest of all for Foyt to achieve because he had to keep up with the new turbine cars—one of which was driven by Parnelli Jones, an outstanding Indy veteran. Jones dropped out of the race only three laps from the finish, clearing the way for A.J. But before Foyt crossed the line, he had to avoid the wreckage of a smashup on the course.

Just a week-and-a-half after his third Indy victory, Foyt teamed with Dan Gurney in the 24 Hours of Le Mans (France) sportscar race. Driving a Ford Mark IV, they became the first all-American

Career Highlights

Seven-time USAC-CART national champion (1960, 1961, 1963, 1964, 1967, 1975, 1979)

First driver in history to win four Indianapolis 500 races (1961, 1964, 1967, 1977)

Only driver in history to win the Indy 500, Daytona 500 (1972) and 24 Hours of Le Mans (1967 with Dan Gurney)

Retired in 1993 as all-time CART wins leader with 67

team to win the international competition. Their average speed of more than 135 miles per hour set a record for the race.

From 1963, A.J. Foyt also appeared in the Winston Cup Grand National competition of the National Association for Stock Car Auto Racing (NASCAR). In 1964 and 1965, he won the Firecracker 400 at the International Speedway in Daytona Beach, Florida. In 1970, he drove to victory in the Winston Western 500 at Riverside, California.

The following two years were Foyt's best in Winston Cup competition. He captured the 1971 Atlanta 500. In both 1971 and 1972, he took the Los Angeles Times 500 at the Ontario Motor Speedway in California. Foyt also won the Daytona 500 in 1972, driving a 1971 Mercury to a record average speed of 161.55 miles per hour.

In USAC competition, A.J. Foyt began to pick up steam in 1973. He became the first person ever to win four 500-mile National

Championship races. Adding to his three victories at Indianapolis, he captured the Schaefer 500 at Pocono (Pennsylvania) International Speedway.

The year 1975 proved to be one of the biggest of Foyt's career. He captured seven USAC Championship Trail races, including the California 500 and the Schaefer 500, and earned over $350,000. He also won the USAC driving title for the sixth time and was named Driver of the Year. (He won his five previous USAC Championships in 1960, 1961, 1963, 1964, and 1967.)

"I don't think I'm pressing my luck by still driving," Foyt said. "I don't try to get into that position on a racetrack where I'm taking any foolish chances. I've learned by getting hurt that if things aren't going right, another day will come."

Foyt continued to show young drivers a thing or two through the 1976 season. He won the 1975–76 International Race of Champions (IROC) series and

A.J. Foyt smiles after winning both of the Twin 150 races at Texas World Speedway in 1976. Proving his all-round driving skills, he won the first 150-mile race in an Indy-type car, and the second 150-mile race in a stock car.

captured second place at the 1976 Indianapolis 500. But his greatest achievement of the year came at College Station, Texas, in the Twin 150 races. He won both the stock-car and the Championship-car events on the same day.

Another Record Broken

Then in 1977, he won his record fourth Indianapolis 500, passing three-time winners Louis Meyer, Mauri Rose, and Wilbur Shaw. In 1979, Foyt won five USAC races and captured his seventh national championship.

Foyt was the only driver to win more than 150 USAC-sponsored races. He collected at least 20 victories in each of the four major USAC divisions—championship, stock, sprint, and midget. In addition, he won seven NASCAR races.

Foyt was known for his quick temper and tough talk. Some said that his temper helped make him a better driver. "The more angry A.J. gets, the faster he drives," said fellow racer Gordon Johncock. But Foyt was also noted for his cool, patient, and precise driving style. A.J.'s greatest rival, Mario Andretti, stated, "I've never, ever, seen Foyt do anything foolish out on a racetrack. Never."

In 1990, Foyt sustained serious injuries in an accident at Elkhart Lake, Wisconsin. His feet and legs were crushed. It took several months of rehabilitation, but he recovered.

A lover of racehorses as well as racecars, he spent a good deal of time at his Texas ranch. In 1992, A.J. Foyt made his 35th consecutive start at the Indianapolis 500. In 1994, at the inaugural Brickyard 400, A.J. drove in his last NASCAR Winston Cup race.

In 2000, A.J. Foyt tied for Driver of the Century (with Mario Andretti) in polling by the Associated Press.

Further Study

"A.J. Foyt," *Foyt Racing.* Online at www.foytracing.com/AJFoyt/aj_bio.html (October 2006)

Wilker, Josh. *A.J. Foyt.* New York, NY: Chelsea House Publishers, 1996.

♟ Frazier, Joe

Joe Frazier (1944–   ), boxer, was born in Beaufort, South Carolina. The second-youngest of 13 children, Frazier quit high school to go north. He eventually got a job in a Philadelphia slaughterhouse. While working out at the 23rd Street Police Athletic League in Philadelphia, he was spotted by Yancey "Yank" Durham, a local trainer of professional boxers and the man who later managed Frazier's career. Frazier captured the national Golden Gloves titles in 1963 and 1964 and won the heavyweight gold medal at the 1964 Olympics. A year later, Frazier launched his professional boxing career. After Muhammad Ali was forced to give up his world heavyweight crown in 1967, the championship picture became confusing. Then on March 8, 1971, at Madison Square Garden, Frazier met Ali, who had made

a comeback. It was billed as "The Fight of the Century," and Frazier retained his title in a thrilling 15-rounder. He suffered his first pro defeat at the hands of George Foreman in January 1973, and lost the crown. "Smokin' Joe" Frazier decided to retire from boxing after failing in a comeback attempt in 1981.

Rubin Frazier used to say to his youngest son, "When you grow up, you're going to be the second Joe Louis."

His son never really became a "second Joe Louis," but Rubin Frazier was not too far off. Joe Frazier did become heavyweight champion of the world, and before he lost his title, he was the winner of boxing's biggest spectacle ever. That historic bout on March 8, 1971, against Muhammad Ali quickly became known as "The Fight of the Century."

"Smokin' Joe" Frazier was the nearest thing to a non-stop puncher that the heavyweight division had ever seen. He outpounded Ali, who, with lightning-fast hands and a dancing shuffle, was the fighting hero of many.

Weighing in at 215½ pounds, Frazier is ready to defend his heavyweight title in a 1972 bout with Terry Daniels.

Frazier, Joe

Millions all over the world watched on closed-circuit television as Frazier beat the idol—winning a unanimous decision over Ali before the largest indoor fight crowd in history. Joe Frazier had come a long way in 27 years.

The Early Years

Joe Frazier was born January 17, 1944, the 12th of 13 children of Rubin and Dolly Frazier. His home was a wood-frame farmhouse in Beaufort, South Carolina—a poor out-of-the-way area where disease and hunger were common.

Wearing a rubber liner under his outfit, Frazier sweats it out during a light workout at his training site in Lake Tahoe, California. He trained there for his 1970 title bout with Bob Foster.

Rubin Frazier and his youngest son always had a close relationship. At 6, Joe worked in the fields serving as "left-hand man" for his father, who had lost an arm in a shotgun accident before the youngster was born.

At 9, Joe Frazier was winning neighborhood fights and dreaming of fulfilling his father's prophecy. He made a punching bag from an old flour sack filled with sand, hung it in a shed, an spent many hours thumping away at it.

Fighting caused him to be expelled from the ninth grade, and he began working in construction. Before his 16th birthday, he married a local girl, Florence Smith. A year later, in 1960, their son Marvis was born. With a family to support

Singing and dancing with his band, The Knockouts, at Philadelphia Veterans Stadium, Frazier performs before a game between the Phillies and the Chicago Cubs in 1971.

and little work in Beaufort, Frazier took a train to Philadelphia. There, he found a job in a slaughterhouse and was able to send for his family. In later years, his family grew to include four daughters.

Frazier had a weight problem. He stood 5 feet, 11 inches, but weighed almost 240 pounds. He began to work out at a Philadelphia Police Athletic League (PAL) gym, a boxing center. Soon, the instructor, Duke Dugent, took notice of the determined boy and asked Yancey "Yank" Durham, a local trainer of pro boxers, for his opinion. Durham watched Frazier,

The battle is on between Joe Frazier and Jimmy Ellis during their 1970 fight for the heavyweight championship of the world at Madison Square Garden.

then pointed out his assets: "The kid could punch, and he kept coming back to the gym. He didn't get discouraged like most of them."

The Olympics

As Frazier's excess pounds were converted into solid muscle, Dugent started him on amateur cards, as arranged boxing matches were called. Weighing a trim 195 pounds, Frazier won Golden Gloves titles in 1963 and 1964.

His unbeaten string came to an end when he fought a giant 300-pounder from Michigan, Buster Mathis, during the finals of the 1964 Olympic trials. Mathis outpointed Joe to win the heavyweight berth on the team. But then Frazier got lucky.

As runner-up, Frazier thus became an alternate. He and Mathis were matched again in San Francisco. Once more Frazier was outpointed, but during the fight Mathis broke a bone in his right hand. The officials chose Frazier to substitute for Mathis at the 1964 Olympics.

In the end, it was a break for the United States, too, for Frazier was the only U.S. gold medalist in boxing at the Tokyo Games. He did it despite a broken left thumb, which had been hurt during the semifinals. He kept the injury secret and managed to defeat Germany's Hans Huber in the finals with only one good hand, getting a narrow decision.

Going Professional

Frazier could ill afford the injury. With his hand in a cast, he could neither turn pro nor work at his old job. Finally, the gold medalist went to work as a janitor in a Philadelphia church. In the spring he began training again, and on August 16, 1965, he made his professional debut, knocking out

Elwood Goss in 1 minute and 42 seconds.

His next time out, a fighter named Mike Bruce hit him on the chin and Frazier went down, but Joe climbed off the canvas to flatten Bruce in the third round. Following the Bruce fight, he quickly scored two more knockouts, convincing Yank Durham that he had possibilities.

Durham needed backers for Frazier. He found them in a group of 40 Philadelphia businessmen, contractors, clergymen, doctors, and lawyers who formed Cloverlay, Inc. Eighty shares were sold at $250 each. Within 19 months there were 270 stockholders, and the original shares on Frazier were

Frazier, Joe

worth $3600 each. Later, both figures were more than doubled.

The group paid Frazier a salary and helped him with investments and other outside interests. Durham chose Frazier's opponents. In 1966 after 11 straight knockouts, Durham sent Frazier to Madison Square Garden against Oscar Bonavena of Argentina, his first rated opponent. Joe won the fight in a split decision.

Eddie Machen was next. The veteran Californian was stopped in the 10th round. Doug Jones and George Chuvalo also failed to go the distance, and Frazier finished the year 1967 with 19 straight wins—all but two by knockouts.

Frazier and Ali

Frazier was a good boxer, but Muhammad Ali was the champ.

Ali stood larger than life. A media magnet, he was quotable, pretty, and controversial. The 1960s were a time of social change. America was mired in an unpopular war in Vietnam, the civil rights movement was in full swing, and staid social conventions were being assailed by a new generation of Americans. Ali fed the fire. He converted to Islam and changed his name from Cassius Clay to Muhammad Ali; he was a vocal opponent of racial injustice; and, to the shock of conservative America, he refused induction into the Army. "I ain't got no quarrel with them Viet Cong," Ali said. He was arrested, convicted, and stripped of his title. He was also refused a boxing license. Facing jail, Ali appealed his conviction, and looked for a way to get back in the ring.

Frazier, on the other hand was less controversial. He read

Training for his title bout with Muhammad Ali in 1971, Frazier has his hands taped by trainer Yank Durham.

the Bible, did his job, liked to sing, and didn't voice his opinions about the war. Many middle-Americans identified with Frazier's more traditional values.

While Ali was on the sidelines watching his court case make its way to the U.S. Supreme Court the World Boxing Association (WBA) was setting up tournaments to crown a new champion. Frazier ranked first in the title claim, but his manager held him back. Said Durham, "Let them fight it out and I [meaning Frazier] will fight the winner." It was a risky stand, but Cloverlay's directors backed Durham.

The WBA tournament ran without Frazier. Meanwhile, he signed to meet his old rival, Buster Mathis—unbeaten in 23 pro fights. The bout on March 4, 1968, highlighted the first boxing

"The kid could punch, and he kept coming back to the gym. He didn't get discouraged like most of them."

—amateur trainer Yank Durham, recalling Joe Frazier's youth

show in the new Madison Square Garden. In the 11th round, Frazier put Mathis on his back for a nine-count, and the fight was stopped. Frazier now was recognized as the heavyweight champion in four states (New York, Massachusetts, Illinois, and Maine).

Frazier went on to defend the "title" against Mexico's Manuel Ramos, Bonavena, Texan Dave Zyglewicz, and Jerry Quarry. The up-and-coming boxer ended up being named Fighter of the Year in 1969 by the Boxing Writers Association.

Jimmy Ellis had won the WBA tournament in 1968, and on February 16, 1970, the two heavyweight title contenders met to settle the dispute. Frazier unloaded his left hook in the fourth round, and Ellis went down twice. Scoring a technical knockout in

Chatting with inmates at the Ohio State Penitentiary in 1971, Frazier talked with television host Phil Donahue and answered questions from the prisoners.

the fifth round, Frazier became the undisputed world heavyweight champion.

But still the shadow of Muhammad Ali haunted Frazier.

The Fight of the Century

Ali, undefeated and still in his prime, considered Frazier a pretender. To him, and many of his fans, Ali was still the champ. To settle the score, Frazier would have to fight Ali. When Ali's license was reinstated they signed for a showdown. The stage was set for the greatest fight of the 20th century.

The fight was preceded by a war of words. Ali called Frazier

Muhammad Ali falls to the canvas after receiving a blow to the jaw from Frazier in the 15th round of their highly publicized 1971 title fight at Madison Square Garden in New York. Frazier won a unanimous decision and successfully defended the heavyweight championship.

"ugly," a "gorilla," and an "Uncle Tom." Frazier, quiet and confident, saved his energy for the ring.

Finally, on March 8, 1971, "Smokin'" Joe Frazier (26–0, with 23 knockouts) met "float like a butterfly, sting like a bee" Muhammad Ali (31–0, with 25 knockouts) in New York's Madison Square Garden for the heavyweight championship of the world.

All eyes turned to New York. Not since 1938 when Joe Louis defeated Max Schmeling in Yankee Stadium had a fight generated as much excitement. The atmosphere was electric. The Garden was sold out a month in advance. An estimated 300 million people watched on closed-circuit television. Reporters from around the globe scrambled for press credentials: over 700 got in, hundreds were turned away. Celebrities sat

Frazier, Joe

Joe and Mark Durham hold buttons kicking off the 1972 Yancey Durham Jr. National Sickle Cell Anemia Foundation's campaign against the disease. Mark, the son of Frazier's manager, Yancy Durham, was a victim of sickle cell anemia.

ringside. Tension filled the arena as everyone waited in breathless anticipation for the fight to begin.

Once it did, they were not disappointed. The fighters came out punching, each determined to claim the crown. Each willing to sacrifice everything they had in the ring.

They fought at a furious pace. Frazier delivered punch after punishing punch to Ali's body. Ali responded with lightening quick jabs and left-right combinations. Ali had a strong 9th round, but late in the 11th Smokin' Joe landed a hook that buckled Ali's knees and sent him staggering into the ropes. Some thought it was over, but Ali survived.

For three more rounds they battled. Then, in the 15th, Frazier landed a devastating left hook that lifted Ali off his feet and sent him careening to the canvas. Ali was down, but not out. Showing incredible courage, he got up to finish the fight.

But the damage was done, Joe Frazier won a unanimous decision and stood alone as the undisputed heavyweight champion.

The world was stunned. Frazier had beaten Ali.

The Aftermath

Easy days followed, and Frazier had time and money to devote himself to his family, a newly purchased farm in South Carolina, his cars and motorcycles, and his blues-rock group called The Knockouts.

In January 1973, Joe lost his title to George Foreman. Joe was decked six times in less than two rounds, and the referee declared a technical knockout (TKO).

Hoping to regain a shot at the heavyweight crown, Frazier fought Ali in a non-title bout in January 1974. Ali won the match with a unanimous decision. After defeating Jerry Quarry and Jimmy Ellis, Joe faced Ali for the third time in the "Thrilla in Manila" held in Manila, the Philippines, on October 1, 1975. Ali won the brutal contest, scoring a 14th-round TKO.

Joe fought two more times before retiring with a fantastic career record of 32–4–1 with 27 KOs. He was named to the International Boxing Hall of Fame in 1990.

Career Highlights

Captured the amateur Golden Gloves title in 1963 and 1964

Won the heavyweight gold medal at the 1964 Summer Olympics

Became undisputed heavyweight champion in 1970

Defended his heavyweight title by defeating Muhammad Ali in 1971

Held the heavyweight title from 1970 to 1973

Compiled a record of 32–4–1 with 27 KOs

> *"When I go out there, I have no pity on my opponent.*
> *I'm out there to win."*
> *—Joe Frazier*

Frazier attempts to land some blows as heavyweight champion Muhammad Ali covers up in the "Thrilla in Manila." Although Joe suffered a TKO in the 14th round of that 1975 bout, the fight was considered one of the best ever.

Joe Frazier's son Marvis kept the family name alive in boxing circles in later years, compiling a 34–2 record with losses only to Mike Tyson and Larry Holmes. His daughter Jacqui also had success in the ring in female competition.

In 2000, the cable network HBO produced a documentary, *One Nation—Divisible,* about the 1971 Ali-Frazier fight at New York's Madison Square Garden. The documentary drew rave reviews for its insightful look at the fight and its influence on American political culture.

Further Study

BOOKS
Knapp, Ron. *Top 10 Heavyweight Boxers.* Springfield, NJ: Enslow Publishers, 1997.

WEB SITES
"Joe Frazier," *International Boxing Hall of Fame.* Online at www.ibhof.com/frazier.htm (October 2006)

Freeman, David

David Freeman (1920–2001), badminton player, was born in Pasadena, California. He attended Pomona College, where he won letters in track and tennis. Freeman first made a national name for himself in tennis. He was the national junior champion in both singles and doubles in 1937. Freeman became even a greater badminton player—and possibly the best ever. Freeman did not lose a singles match from 1939 to his semiretirement in 1949. He won all the U.S. singles matches from 1939 through 1948 and came out of retirement to win again in 1953. He also won the All-England championship, which served as the unofficial world championship, in 1949. He became the first American to win the coveted title. Freeman

was known in badminton for his incredible defensive play. In 1956, Freeman, by then a doctor, was elected to the Helms Badminton Hall of Fame. David Freeman died on June 28, 2001. An annual badminton tournament is held in his name in San Diego, California.

No matter what type of racket he used, David Freeman used it well. With a ping-pong paddle, 13-year-old David won his first table tennis trophy in 1934. In 1937, gripping a tennis racket, David Freeman won the United States Junior National Tennis Championships in both the singles and doubles events. But it was his almost unbelievable skill with the badminton racket that earned Freeman his lasting fame.

From 1939 until his final retirement from tournament play in 1953, David Freeman never lost a singles match in badminton.

Badminton was originally a native game of India called "poona." Adopted by officers of the British Army in the 1860s, the sport found its way to England.

In 1873, it was first presented to British society during a party given at Badminton, the country estate of the Duke of Beaufort. The sport was then called "the game that was played at Badmin-

ton," and gradually the name was shortened to "badminton."

As the game increased in popularity, many badminton clubs were formed, making it necessary to standardize the playing rules. By the late 1880s and 1890s, this had been done. The All-England championship for men began in 1899, and a year later women had their own championships. These competitions became official in 1904.

By the end of World War II (1939–45), the sport had become so popular in England that there were more than 9000 badminton clubs spread throughout the country.

By 1929, badminton began to catch on in the United States. But it was not until 1949 that an American, David Freeman, became the first and only one of his countrymen to capture the All-England title.

The Early Years

David Guthrie Freeman was born September 6, 1920, in Pasadena, California. His family was well educated; his father was a Presbyterian minister, his mother was a professor of religion at Occidental College. Freeman seemed to follow his parents' interest in academics. He was an excellent student and became a very well-rounded person. After graduation from Pasadena High School in 1938, David Freeman attended

Pomona College for premedical studies. There he won letters in tennis and track and sang in the glee club. He was elected president of the student body in his senior year. Following his graduation in 1942, Freeman went on to Harvard University to study medicine. He received his medical degree in 1945.

He next spent two years in a U.S. Army training course. He interned at San Diego Hospital and then was attached to the Army Medical Corps in the Panama

Canal Zone. After his discharge, David Freeman studied neurosurgery at the University of Michigan. He established a medical practice in San Diego.

During the busy years David Freeman spent in college and medical school, he was also a remarkably active badminton competitor. The "Pasadena Flash," as he was called, was described as having the "speed of a projectile" and uncanny accuracy of placement. These skills helped the

Freeman, David

speedster win his first U.S. badminton singles title in 1939.

The next year he again won the singles title. Then he added both the doubles title, with Chester Goss, and the mixed doubles title, with Sally (Sara) Williams (later, Sara Williams Skibbins)—a clean sweep of available crowns. Freeman repeated his capture of the three titles again in 1941 and 1942—a remarkable feat—before the championships were suspended from 1943 through 1946 because of World War II.

After the War

Returning to badminton competition in 1947, Freeman regained his U.S. titles in both the singles and men's doubles events (with Web-ster Kimball). Freeman went on six weeks later to win the Army's Sheridan Cup tennis title as well. The next year, 1948, he won his sixth straight singles title and, with Wynn Rogers as his partner, won his fifth straight doubles title.

The 1949 All-England championship is considered a classic in badminton history. Freeman played against two Malaysians, Ooi Teik Hock and Womg Peng Soon, then thought to be the world's best players. But the combination of self-confidence, speed, judgment, superb concentration, and extraordinary stamina that the young U.S. player brought to that series could not be beaten.

With incredible stamina and quickness, Freeman lunges for a near-impossible shot.

After the 1949 match, he retired from active competition to concentrate on neurosurgery. His retirement came after winning every singles match he had entered during the previous 11 years.

Not Finished Yet

But he was not yet finished. David Freeman emerged from retirement in 1953 and recaptured the U.S. men's singles title for the seventh time before retiring again. In addition to his seven singles titles, Freeman was the holder of five doubles titles and three mixed doubles crowns. He was unbeaten

Dr. David Freeman smiles after winning another national badminton championship.

in Thomas Cup play (badminton's equivalent to the Davis Cup) in 1948 and 1949. He was elected to the Helms Badminton Hall of Fame in 1956.

His family and his career became his focus, but he continued to be involved in competitive badminton—he was on hand each year to present the trophies at the David Freeman Open Tournament held each year in San Diego.

Career Highlights

Won the U.S. Junior National Tennis Championships in both singles and doubles competition in 1937

Did not lose a match from 1939 to 1949

Victorious at the 1949 All-England championship, becoming the first American to ever win the tournament

Elected to the Helms Badminton Hall of Fame in 1956

An annual tournament is held each year in his honor

Gable, Dan

Dan Gable (1948–), wrestler, was born in Waterloo, Iowa. Gable began wrestling in junior high school and wasted no time establishing himself as a winner. He was unbeaten in all three years of varsity wrestling in high school and won the Iowa interscholastic championship title three times. Gable continued his perfect record throughout his sophomore and junior years at Iowa State University. Among his victories were the National Collegiate Athletic Association (NCAA) titles in 1968 and 1969. It was not until the last meet of his senior year, in the NCAA championships, that he lost for the first time. Before that loss, Gable had won 181 consecutive matches during his prep and college careers. In 1971, he won the world championship at 149.5 pounds. Dan avenged his only loss when he defeated Larry Owings to make the U.S. Olympic

team in 1972. At Munich, West Germany, Gable won the Olympic gold medal to top off his brilliant career. Dan Gable was recognized by many as the greatest amateur wrestler in U.S. history. He became head coach at the University of Iowa in 1977 and before long was regarded as the nation's most successful wrestling coach.

The capacity crowd attending the 1970 National Collegiate Athletic Association (NCAA) wrestling tournament in McGaw Hall at Northwestern University sat in stunned disbelief. They had just seen Dan Gable of Iowa State go down to defeat at the hands of Larry Owings of the University of Washington. After winning 181 matches in a row, one of the most outstanding wrestlers in the United States had suffered his first loss.

Dan Gable—born October 25, 1948—started wrestling while still in junior high school. At West High School in Waterloo, Iowa, Dan was undefeated for three straight years in varsity competition. He won the Iowa State High School Championship in his weight division three years in a row.

He continued his great wrestling record at Iowa State, where he came within 30 seconds of being the only wrestler ever to

go undefeated through both his high school and college wrestling career.

Gable won the NCAA 130-pound wrestling title in 1968 as a sophomore and the NCAA 137-pound title in 1969 as a junior. In that year he was also named the outstanding wrestler of the tournament. Next, he breezed through another undefeated season as a senior. At the time of the 1970 tournament, everyone expected him to carry off the 142-pound championship.

The Waterloo, Iowa, native reached the finals as expected. He had one match to go, having now won 181 straight matches during high school and college. With 30 seconds to go in this final match against Larry Owings, the Iowa Stater was ahead on points. Then Owings suddenly scored four quick points. For the first time in his wrestling career, Dan Gable was the loser.

Not a Quitter

Dan lost, but he did not quit. He may have been shocked the night of his defeat, but that did not sidetrack him from his greatest goal. That goal was to win an Olympic gold medal in wrestling.

Just two weeks after the loss, he entered the national Amateur Athletic Union (AAU) tournament. Not only was he the winner of his weight division, but he was also voted the outstanding wrestler of that tournament.

For the next three years, the determined wrestler spent most of his time working toward the Olympic gold medal. He devoted well over 40 hours every week to training. Even more important, he practiced conditioning exercises at every chance.

Some experts felt that Gable would be a sure winner—not because he was more skilled than other grapplers, but because he was in better condition.

As Gable put it, "International matches consist of three three-minute periods, and lots of time after the first period the score will be close or I'll be behind. But after that, I often feel the other guy wearing out and then I get him.

Career Highlights

Won the Iowa state title 3 consecutive times

Posted undefeated records en route to 2 consecutive NCAA titles (1968, 1969)

Won 181 consecutive matches during his high school and college career

Captured the world championship at 149.5 pounds in 1971

Emerged victorious at the 1972 Olympics, winning the gold medal

As head coach, guided the University of Iowa to 11 NCAA national championships

"I'm a big believer in starting with high standards and raising them. We make progress only when we push ourselves to the highest level. If we don't progress, we backslide into bad habits, laziness and poor attitude."

—Dan Gable, on the importance of setting goals

Gable, Dan

Larry Owings (kneeling) of Washington breaks a hold and flips Gable of Iowa State in their final match of the 1970 NCAA wrestling championships. Owings won the match and the 142-pound class title to give Gable his first loss ever.

Foreign wrestlers aren't like our guys. Once you get ahead of them, they almost always quit."

For international competition, Gable had to learn some new rules. Amateur wrestlers from other countries start using international rules in their schools during their formative years. The young American had been wrestling under collegiate rules in the United States for most of his life. These rules are much different from international rules.

But Gable did have help. Besides his burning desire and his full-time training program, he had the full support of both his parents. His father and mother had always been 100 percent behind his wrestling career and gave Dan the support and encouragement he needed.

Preparing for the Olympics

The Gable family knew that if Dan was going to win the gold medal in Munich, he would have to defeat the best. And the best in amateur wrestling in those years had been the Russians.

In the three years before the Olympics, Gable wrestled against Russian opponents 10 times in international competition. Each

time he won. As the Olympics approached, the sturdy wrestler remained undefeated in international competition. Despite his perfect record in international competition—which included the gold medal at the Pan American Games in Cali, Colombia, and the world championship at 149.5 pounds in Sofia, Bulgaria, in 1971—he was not automatically a member of the Olympic team.

First of all, he had suffered a serious leg injury. Doctors advised him to undergo surgery on a torn cartilage, but Gable refused to take time off from his training program. "Wrestling with one leg has made me a better wrestler," he maintained. "I've had to find new ways to do things and I've improved a lot."

Gable easily won an Olympic qualifying tournament in Iowa City, pinning all six of his foes. Now came the one big tournament before the Olympics—the U.S.

As head wrestling coach at the University of Iowa, Gable (wearing glasses at left) led the Hawkeyes to nine straight NCAA titles.

Olympic wrestling team trials in Anoka, Minnesota.

There was one other wrestling threat in the 149.5-pound weight division. Another man had also qualified for the trials, and his name was Larry Owings. The only wrestler ever to defeat Gable was going to meet him again. This meeting would be the first between Gable and Owings since the finals of the 1970 NCAA tournament. Could the Olympic hopeful avenge his only loss?

The wrestling fans, packed into the Anoka Senior High School field house, learned the answer during the fifth round of the trials. Gable avenged the lone defeat on his wrestling record by overwhelming Owings 7–1.

Then on to Munich he went. In the 1972 Olympics, the 150-pounder became the first U.S. grappler to win a gold medal in 12 years. Although he suffered a bad cut over his eye in the first round, Gable was never in serious trouble. His only close decision came against Rusan Ashuraliev of Russia, whom Dan defeated by a 3–0 score.

The United States, led by Gable and two other gold medalists—Wayne Wells and Ben Peterson—came through with 32 points in the unofficial freestyle wrestling competition, second only to Russia, the winner with 44 points.

Olympic Gold

In his final competitive match of 1973, Gable easily defeated his Soviet opponent in a U.S.-Russian meet. Gable retired from wrestling with an Olympic gold medal and one of the most impressive individual records in history.

Dan did not end his dedication to wrestling, however. Knowing that his conditioning program had played a major role in his success, he became supervisor of physical fitness at the University of Iowa.

He also served as the school's assistant wrestling coach. Gable became head coach in 1977. Through 1997, his dual-meet record was 355–21–5. He led Iowa to 21 Big Ten championships in 21 years and 11 NCAA titles, including 9 in consecutive years (1978–86). Only two other teams in college sports history (Yale golf, 1905–13 and Southern Cal track, 1935–43) had won nine consecutive titles.

He coached 152 All-Americans, 45 national champions, 106 Big-Ten Champions, and 10 Olympians (4 of whom won gold medals); under his leadership the 1984 Olympic team won 7 gold medals. He was selected as head coach for the 1999 World Championships and the 2000 Olympic team. Dan Gable's success as a wrestler and coach has been among the greatest in the history of the sport.

Further Study

BOOKS

Zavoral, Norman. *A Season on the Mat: Dan Gable and the Pursuit of Perfection.* New York, NY: Simon and Schuster, 1998.

WEB SITES

"College Wrestling: Dan Gable," *Iowa Public Television.* Online at www.collegewrestling.iptv.org/dan.cfm (October 2006)

🥍 Gait, Gary

Gary Gait (1967–   ), lacrosse player, and his identical twin brother Paul were born in Victoria, British Columbia, Canada. Gary and Paul began playing lacrosse early, and both became great. They led their hometown team, the Esquimalt Legion, to four straight British Columbia provincial championships (1985–88) and the national title (1988). Next, they dominated lacrosse at Syracuse University, where Gary became the school's all-time leading scorer and was first-team All-American three times. The Gait brothers became professional lacrosse players in 1991, when Gary was named Rookie of the Year. Gait retired in 2006 after helping the Canadians win the 2006 World Lacrosse Championship.

The Syracuse Orangemen were playing Penn in the semifinals of the NCAA lacrosse tournament. Gary Gait took the ball behind the net. Suddenly, a gasp came from the crowd. People stared in disbelief. The officials, confused and bewildered, scratched their heads. From the sidelines, the Penn bench was in an uproar. In the press booth reporters frantically analyzed the replay. Did they just see what they thought they saw?

Early Years

Gary Gait and his twin brother Paul were born April 5, 1967, in Victoria, British Columbia. Gary is older by three minutes. The boys began playing lacrosse at age four. By age 12, Gait had won his first age-group national championship.

The Gaits were good at lacrosse, but they had to persevere to succeed. The Minto Cup is given to the Canadian junior champions. Said Gait, "While growing up in Canada I lost the Minto Cup four years in a row and then finally won it my final year—1988." What drove him in the early days to excel? "I loved to compete! I grew up with my identical brother and we competed at everything."

Gary Gait's competitive spirit would drive him to the pinnacle of his sport.

Baggataway Roots of Lacrosse

The modern game of lacrosse developed from a wild and unorganized sport played originally by Indian tribes in Canada. The Indians called their game *baggataway*. In baggataway, the field was unlimited, sometimes covering several miles of terrain. To many Indians, the ball was a sacred object symbolizing the sun or the moon. Consequently, the hand was never permitted to touch the ball.

Colorado Mammoth's Gary Gait plays in his final home game before retiring. Gait is known as the Michael Jordan of lacrosse.

> *"If you have passion for the sport and put in the work, you will be successful."*
>
> —*Gary Gait*

Gait, Gary

The 1911 *Encyclopedia Britannica* described the game this way: "In the old days, according to Catlin, warriors of two tribes in their war-paint would form the sides, often 800 or 1000 strong. (Catlin, an American artist known for his paintings of American Indians, lived from 1796 to 1872.) The goals were placed from 500 yards to one-half mile apart with practically no side boundaries. A solemn dance preceded the game, after which the ball was tossed into the air and the two sides rushed to catch it on 'crosses,' similar to those now in use. The medicine-men acted as umpires, and the squaws urged on the men by beating them with switches." The object was to drive the ball under the goal of the opposing team. Running with the ball was permitted after picking it up with the racket.

The French-Canadian pioneers named the game "lacrosse" from the shape of the stick used in playing. The crook-headed rod reminded them of a bishop's long cross, which in French is called a *crozier*. By the mid-1800s, lacrosse clubs had been formed throughout Canada. Around that time, Dr. George W. Beers formed some standard rules—and thus became the "father of lacrosse."

Lacrosse was named the national game of Canada in 1867, the year Canada became a Dominion of Great Britain. It flourished throughout Canada and in the 1880s gained modest popularity along the East Coast of the United States. Consequently, although lacrosse has not been a major sport in many areas of the United States, it has long been popular in the Ivy League and other East Coast schools.

An East Coast Tradition

The modern game of lacrosse is played on a field 60 yards wide with goals 80 yards apart. A five-ounce rubber ball is used. The players handle the ball only with their crosses and may use their bodies to block each other. The 60-minute games are divided into 15-minute quarters, and substitution is allowed. As in ice hockey, some penalties involve the benching of a player for one- to three-minute periods. Generally lacrosse is played on an open field.

One of the first schools to build a lacrosse tradition was Johns Hopkins University. Lacrosse at Hopkins began with the founding of the Johns Hopkins Lacrosse Club in 1882. Among the early stars to play for Hopkins was Dr. Ronald T. Abercrombie. At 5

An illustration by George Catlin of the Native American Tullock-chish-ko (He-who-drinks-the-juice-of-the-stone) who was the most distinguished baggataway player of the Chocktaw nation.

feet, 7 inches, and 140 pounds, Abercrombie captained the 1900 team and gained fame as a center. It is said that he never lost a face-off. However, his influence on the game went far beyond his own play.

In 1898 Abercrombie developed and introduced the short-handled lacrosse stick used by attack players. He also introduced the lacrosse net. He was an evangelist for the sport, encouraging its play at colleges and universities. When the National Intercollegiate Lacrosse Association was established, he became its chairman. In 1904, he wrote an illustrated article, "How to Play Lacrosse." It was the first known explanation of how to play the game.

Indians invented the game, and in 1910, Indian students at the

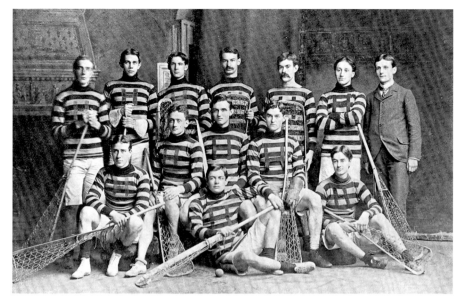

Carlisle Indian Industrial School recaptured the lacrosse spotlight. Founded in 1879, Carlisle was the first off-reservation government boarding school for Indian children. Carlisle's athletic director, the legendary coach "Pop" Warner, replaced baseball with lacrosse as the school's spring sport. "Athletics at Carlisle," said Pop Warner, "are here for the students, not the students here for the athletics." Since lacrosse is an Indian game, Warner expected his students to excel. And excel they did. By 1911, Carlisle was playing against the best teams in the nation, including Johns Hopkins. Olympic hero Jim Thorpe (1888–1953) played lacrosse at the Carlisle Indian School.

Forty years later, another famous athlete, the great Jim Brown, excelled at the game. Brown, who went on to football fame as a running back for the Cleveland Browns, played lacrosse for Syracuse University in the 1950s. Why did he play? "I loved the game," said Brown. "We played because we loved it." In a sport where players typically weigh under 170 pounds, the 6-foot, 2-inch, 235-pound Brown presented an imposing challenge to opposing teams.

Gait, Gary

Next Year, We'll Win

At 6 feet, 1 inch, and about 225 pounds, the Gait brothers are more in the tradition of Jim Brown than Doc Abercrombie. Like Brown, the Gaits played for the Orangemen of Syracuse University. And like Brown, the Gaits had it all: strength, speed, skills, agility, and drive.

In 1987, when Syracuse coach Roy Simmons first saw the brothers on the playing field, he was spellbound. He made them midfielders and gave them the entire run of the field. In their first year as Orangemen, the Gaits advanced to the Final Four but lost to Cornell.

Career Highlights

All-time high scorer at Syracuse University (192)

All-World Team (1990, 1994, 1998)

Six-time MVP of National Lacrosse League (1995–99, 2003)

Four-time MVP of USCLA

All-20th Century Team (*Lacrosse* magazine)

25th Anniversary NCAA Team

Coach Simmons was disappointed, but the Gait boys were undeterred. "Don't worry coach, we've figured this game out," Gary said. "This won't happen again next year. Next year, we'll win."

And they did. The Orangemen, led by Gary Gait and his brother Paul, went on to crush the competition. Syracuse got so good that teams started dropping them from their schedules. With the Gaits on the field, Syracuse grabbed three straight NCAA National Championships (1988, 1989, 1990).

What Was That?

During the 1988 season, the Orangemen faced Penn in the NCAA Final Four. They had played Penn earlier in the season and had trouble beating Penn's zone defense. Penn had figured out how to keep the Gaits from attacking from the front. But, as Paul put it, "We figured out they do not defend behind their goal." But how in the world do you score from behind the goal?

During the match, the world learned how. Gary took the ball behind the net, leaped over the crease line, extended his stick, and jammed the ball into the net from behind. The ball crossed the goal line before his feet touched

Canada's Gary Gait, left, tries to keep possession as he is checked by Finland's Dave Huoppi during action at the World Lacrosse Championships in London, Ontario.

the ground, thereby preventing a crease violation call.

The fans, and the Penn defense, were flabbergasted. Protests rang out from the Penn bench. But the goal stood. It is considered one of the most spectacular and inventive moves in lacrosse history. Fans dubbed it the "Air Gait," and Gary became the Michael Jordan of lacrosse.

The move was so devastating that the NCAA ultimately amended the rule book to outlaw it.

When his college career ended Gary Gait had scored 192 goals, putting him second to Stan Cockerton on the all-time NCAA scoring list. He was a four-time All-American, two-time NCAA Player of the Year (1988 and 1990), and the 1990 NCAA Tournament Outstanding Player.

What Next?

College lacrosse is a respected sport with a rich tradition. Professional lacrosse is a sideline sport with low pay. Unfortunately, some people considered it a kind of joke. But if you wanted to play lacrosse after college, this was your only option.

When the Gait brothers graduated, they were both drafted into the Major Indoor Lacrosse League (later the National Lacrosse

League). Gary quickly made his mark with his new team, the Detroit Turbos, earning Rookie of the Year honors in 1991.

The Gait brothers began to change professional lacrosse for the better. Their style of play was based on skill and finesse, not violence, and the rest of the league began to follow their example.

The Gaits brought legitimacy to the sport and helped gain the attention of sponsors. "None of the manufacturers had players representing them. That was non-existent. Team sponsorship wasn't really existent," Gary Gait recalled. The Gait brothers were the first to win endorsement deals from lacrosse equipment manufacturers.

Over the next 15 seasons Gary Gait made professional lacrosse better in every way. He was named Most Valuable Player (MVP) six times. He retired as the league's all-time leading scorer with the most career regular season goals (563), most career regular season points (1010) and most career post-season goals (65). In 2006, he went on to coach the Colorado Mammoth to its first league title.

The Icing on the Cake

Throughout his spectacular career one goal had eluded him: a World Lacrosse Championship. In 2006, in his last game ever, the 39-year-old Gary Gait found himself playing for a final chance at that one remaining title. Gait scored four goals in the last quarter to lead Canada to an historic win over the United States. It was a storybook finish to a remarkable career. "I've been playing lacrosse for 27 years," said Gait. "This is unbelievable. It was a thrill to win in our home country, in front of our fans."

"You can compare him to Michael Jordan in basketball or Wayne Gretzky in hockey," Portland Lumber Jax lacrosse coach Derek Keenan said. "He was all of that, for sure. He was big, strong, fast, and powerful, with an unbelievable skill level. He did things with a stick that few have ever done."

Ask any college lacrosse coach who was the best ever, and you might hear the names Jim Thorpe or Jim Brown, but give them a minute to reflect and they will probably say Gary Gait.

Further Study

Fisher, Donald M. *Lacrosse: A History of the Game.* Baltimore: Johns Hopkins University Press, 2002.

"Hall of Fame Biography: Gary Gait," U.S. Lacrosse. Online at www.uslacrosse. org/museum/hofbios/gait_gary.phtml (November 2006)

Lupton, Andrew "Closing the Gait." National Post. Online at www.canada. com/nationalpost/news/sports/story. html?id=944afd9a-f416-43ec-8296-71f4bab22793 (November 2006)

⊙ Garlits, Don

Don Garlits (1932–   ), race driver, was born in Tampa, Florida. He worked on cars as a youth and became a mechanic after leaving high school. After driving briefly in modified stock cars on small, oval dirt tracks, Garlits turned to drag racing. He won his first major victory at the National Hot Rod Association (NHRA) "Safety Safari" in 1955. Don continued to win races and also gained fame for his innovative designs, including the rear-engine dragster. Garlits captured six International Hot Rod Association

(IHRA) world championships and 10 world titles in the American Hot Rod Association (AHRA). In 1986, he became the first drag racer to reach the 270-mile-per-hour mark for the quarter mile. By 1988, he had won 35 NHRA Top Fuel titles. Don "Big Daddy" Garlits is considered the father of modern competitive drag racing.

After winning his sixth U.S. Nationals title in 1984, 52-year-old Don "Big Daddy" Garlits said, "This is my biggest victory. Because of my age, I'm not supposed to be able to do this." His win was not a fluke, but the beginning of one of the most successful stretches of his career.

The next year, Big Daddy won 6 of 13 National Hot Rod Association (NHRA) Top Fuel events—a record for single-season victories. He again took the U.S. Nationals and captured his third NHRA world championship. In 1986, he became the first Top Fuel racer to win the world championship in

consecutive years. He also became the first to take three straight U.S. Nationals.

Garlits set the fastest speed in drag racing history with a 272.56 mile per hour (mph) mark in 1986 (though this record was later broken). The most successful Top Fuel drag racer in history, Don Garlits won more races and brought in more new ideas than any other competitor.

Don Garlits was born on January 14, 1932, in Tampa, Florida. The Depression was just about at its worst and his family was having a hard time. His father

had been an engineer with the Westinghouse Corporation. He had moved the family to Florida because of his health. He raised chickens and grew oranges and, until the Depression years, things had gone well.

Then a bank failure wiped out the family savings and their orchard was destroyed by fruit flies. The Garlits family was reduced to poverty. When Don was 11, his parents separated. Don then lived

---

Garlits's innovations and designs have paved the way for faster, safer, and more powerful cars.

with his mother, who remarried when he was 12.

Don and his brother milked a herd of 30 cows twice a day on their stepfather's farm. The boys spent their time going to school, running the dairy, and taking care of the farm machinery and the farm truck. As they got older, the farm chores seemed easier and Don and Ed spent a lot of their free time building balsa- and tissue-paper model airplanes and repairing bicycles.

Don studied accounting in high school. After he finished high school, he worked for a while in an accounting job. Later, he gave it up so he could get a job working on automobiles. Garlits did not have the goal of becoming a champion drag racer, however, because in 1950 there was no organized drag racing anywhere.

There have always been drivers who wanted to see whose car could get away fastest from a standing start. But racing on public roads was illegal and dangerous to other traffic. In the late 1940s, there had been a big boom in this sport in southern California—on the streets and on dry lake beds. Drag racing on city streets after midnight, using traffic lights as starting signals, was giving the sport a bad name. Something needed to be done.

The First Drag Strips

Finally in July 1950, the California Highway Patrol, working with Wally Parks and others, set up one of the country's first legal and safe drag strips. They marked off 440 yards—a quarter of a mile—on a runway at the Orange County Airport and history's first organized drag race was held.

Within a few months there were dozens of other strips around the country—including one on an old airstrip at Zephyr Hills, Florida, 20 miles from where Don Garlits lived. Drag racing could now develop into a recognized part of auto racing.

One of the rules at some of the strips was that no driver with a bad record of traffic violations could race.

> *"I want to leave something for future generations when I'm gone."*
>
> *—Don Garlits, on his influence in drag racing*

Garlits, Don

For five years, Don Garlits worked as a mechanic, built dragsters, and drove in drag races around Florida. His first big race was at Lake City, Florida, in 1955. The National Hot Rod Association (NHRA), formed in 1951, had picked a group of the best drivers in the new sport and sent them around the country to show local drag racers how it was done. When the tour reached Florida, unknown Don Garlits beat the well-known Joe Travis in an upset victory.

The next year, he put bicycle wheels on the front of his dragster. It was one of a long string of new ideas that Garlits brought to drag racing. Garlits then took the 1956 Florida state championship and he was on his way. In the years that followed, Don Garlits established himself as the undisputed king of drag racing.

In 1964, he won the NHRA National championship at Indianapolis, Indiana, with an elapsed time (ET) of 7.57 seconds and a speed of 198.22 mph. In 1965, "Big Daddy" Garlits won the Bakersfield, California, fuel and gas championships—one of the wins he enjoyed the most. In 1965, he won the NHRA Nationals again, posting an ET of 6.77 and a speed of 220.58 mph. No one else had ever won the Indy Nationals twice. As if that was not enough, Garlits came back in 1968 to win the Nationals for the third time, with an ET of 6.87 and a speed of 226.70 mph. The same year, he also won the AHRA Spring Nationals.

Big Daddy and the unusual cars he designed and built had become the hottest combination in drag racing.

A Special Kind of Driver

Racers like Don Garlits, who race a quarter of a mile from a standing start, are a strange and special kind of competition driver. Garlits says, "We're not really race drivers because we don't have to drive in traffic, vary speeds, pass other drivers in traffic, go around corners. But we need all the tools of the good race driver—determination and courage and quick reflexes. We become race drivers when we get in trouble, like Breedlove at Bonneville."

In a race at Long Beach, California, Garlits's 1600-horsepower, 426 cubic-inch supercharged power plant was too strong for the two-speed gearbox. The gearbox exploded, the car ripped in half, and the driver's half rolled over and over. Both of Garlits's legs were broken, and the toes had to be amputated from his right foot.

A year later, in 1971, he built and raced the first successful rear engine dragster, winning the Winter Nationals at Pomona, California, and the AHRA world championship.

"When something went wrong in a front-engine car with the driver sitting behind the motor, everything happened in front of him," Garlits said, "fire and danger of flying debris. I wanted to build a safer car, so I closed my mind to the failures of others who had tried the rear engine concept."

In 1972, Don Garlits had the best time of the meet in the AHRA Winter Nationals at Lakeland,

Career Highlights

Won his first National Hot Rod Association (NHRA) title in 1955

Captured six International Hot Rod Association world titles

Ten-time American Hot Rod Association national champion

Became the first drag racer to reach the 270 mph mark in 1986

Won 35 NHRA Top Fuel titles, second-most in history

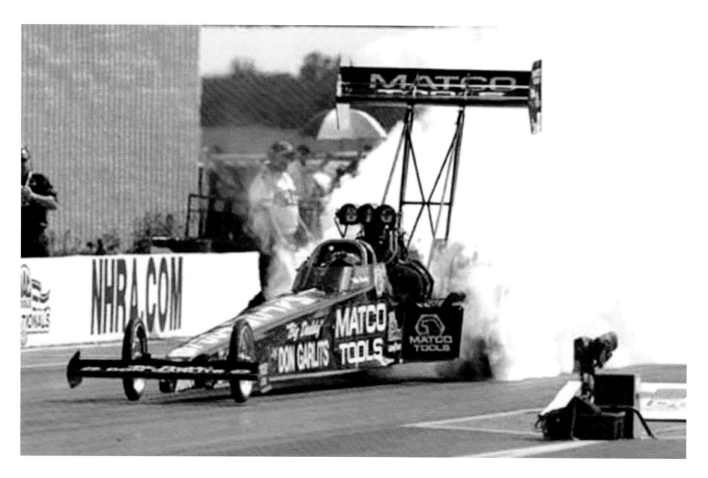

Florida. He also won 6 out of 10 AHRA Grand American races and another AHRA world championship. On March 19, 1972, at the NHRA Gator Nationals, Garlits drove his rear-engine car to an all-time record, with a speed of 243.90 mph and an ET of 6.15 seconds.

He had a world record, but Garlits thought his prize money was not enough. He left the NHRA in protest and in May 1972, he founded the Professional Racers Organization (PRO). Garlits and many other drivers believed that more money would increase the competition and help pay for the cars, which cost as much as $100,000.

In the finals of the 1973 Winter Nationals at Scottsdale, Arizona, Don Garlits drove a new rear-engine, supercharged Dodge hemi-dragster. At the event, he set an AHRA record of 239.60 mph. In 1974, Garlits won the AHRA point standings championship for the fourth time in five years.

Garlits got back into NHRA racing again and did well in 1975. He captured three national events that year and took the world championship in Top Fuel. He also became the first drag racer to reach 250 mph for the quarter mile, with an amazing 250.69 clocking.

Over the years, Garlits was drag racing's chief innovator. His rear-engine design of dragsters revolutionized the sport. He was also responsible for the fire-resistant driving suit. In the 1980s, his Swamp Rat XXX featured a 3000-horsepower engine and an enclosed cockpit. The tiny 13-inch front wheels, only 26 inches apart, were covered by an aerodynamic cowling. The innovative car went on permanent display at the Smithsonian Institution in Washington, D.C., in 1987.

Garlits won his eighth U.S. Nationals Top Fuel title and third NHRA world championship in 1986. By 1988, he had won 35 NHRA Top Fuel titles. The Don "Big Daddy" Garlits Museum of Drag Racing, located just south of Ocala, Florida, opened in 1984.

Further Study

Cockerham, Paul W. *Drag Racing.* Philadelphia, PA: Chelsea House Publishers, 1997.

⊕ Garnett, Kevin

Kevin Garnett (1976–   ), basketball player, was born May 19, 1976, in Mauldin, South Carolina. Garnett has often been labeled the best all-around player in the National Basketball Association (NBA). In 1995, he was drafted fifth overall by the Minnesota Timberwolves. He became the first player in more than 20 years to make the jump directly from high school to the NBA. Nicknamed "K.G." by fans and teammates, Garnett has used his 6-foot, 11-inch frame to become a reliable scoring threat and dominating rebounder. Before he was 30 years old, he was

selected All-NBA six times. Garnett won a gold medal at the 2000 Summer Olympics in Sydney, Australia, as a member of the U.S. Olympic basketball team. The 2003–04 season saw Garnett capture the NBA Most Valuable Player (MVP) award. That season, he averaged 24 points, 14 rebounds, and 5 assists per contest.

In 1995, a tall, slim high school senior prepared to do something that had not been attempted in more than 20 years: jump directly to the NBA. While many NBA scouts and experts criticized the decision, the high school National Player of the Year remained focused on his goal. Kevin Garnett was determined to silence all the doubters.

Early Life

Kevin Garnett was born May 19, 1976, in Mauldin, South Carolina, outside Greenville. He lived with his mother, Shirley Irby Garnett, and two sisters, Sonya and Ashley. Garnett's childhood was both difficult and turbulent. Kevin's biological father, a former high school basketball star named O'Lewis McCollough, was rarely involved in his son's life. The lack of a father figure often made young Kevin upset.

"Everyone has a father in their lives, and he was hurt by that," Shirley Garnett admitted. "It bothered his mind. He once asked me,

'Mom, what do you think it would have been like [to have a dad]?'"

Still, Shirley Garnett did her best to raise her three children on her own. She was strict and vowed to keep Kevin and his sisters away from drugs and violence. She was a practicing Jehovah's Witness, a strict form of Christianity. She tried to instill values in Kevin. "I was way firm," recalled Shirley. "I

Garnett (21) drives to the basket as the Houston Rockets' Maurice Taylor (2) avoids a foul.

Garnett, Kevin

taught him at an early age, I could only give him what he needed, not what he wanted."

Stability on the Court

The one constant in Kevin's life was basketball. He was tall and athletic,

Career Highlights

Became the first player since the 1970s to go directly from high school to NBA

Played on the gold medal–winning Team USA in 2000 Olympics

Named NBA MVP in 2003–04

Received All-NBA selection six times before age 30

Was the first NBA player to earn Player of the Month honors four times in one season

Averaged more than 20 points per game in first 10 years as a professional

Was the first player in Minnesota Timberwolves history to lead the league in a statistical category.

Led the NBA in rebounds in 2003–04

a perfect mix for a basketball player. He grew to love the game and practiced constantly on the playgrounds near his home. He took his skills to Mauldin High School in the fall of 1992. He excelled on the basketball court during his freshman year, averaging more than 12 points and 14 rebounds per game. He even chipped in 7 blocked shots per contest. News of Garnett's skills quickly began to circulate around town and beyond.

By his junior year, Garnett's name was constantly appearing in newspapers and on television broadcasts. College and NBA scouts traveled from outside South Carolina to attend basketball games at Mauldin High School. They wanted to see for themselves what all the sportswriters were raving about.

Young fans ran up to Kevin before and after the games, asking for his autograph. The sports shoe company Nike even invited him to basketball camps they sponsored far away from Mauldin—in Indiana, Oregon, and Illinois. But things weren't perfect for the young athlete. After his junior year, Kevin ran himself into trouble.

A Fresh Start Is Tough

Problems arose following Kevin's junior season at Mauldin High

School. Racial tensions erupted into a fight between white and black students, and Kevin was in the middle of it. The police came, and 17-year-old Garnett was arrested. Some witnesses claimed that Kevin was only an innocent bystander in a racially motivated altercation. Kevin had not been in trouble with the law until now, and his mother was shocked. She recalled, "When someone told me Kevin was arrested, I kind of laughed. I just didn't believe it." In order to escape the controversy, she packed up her family and moved to Chicago.

The following fall, Garnett enrolled at Farragut Academy, a public school on Chicago's west side. The school had a long tradition of basketball success. Kevin already knew the school's coach, William Nelson. The two had met at a Nike summer basketball camp.

Things were tough for the Garnett family. Shirley Garnett rented a single-bedroom apartment for the family of four. They struggled to make ends meet, and often they didn't have enough food to eat. "It was hard, very hard—to eat rice many nights, to go to the grocery store and realize you have only $20 left on your Visa, having to walk when my car was stolen

Farragut Academy coach William Nelson was grateful for Garnett's skills and work ethic. Nelson claims that Garnett made a lasting impression on the school. "Kevin is still here really. I have younger players who saw Kevin working harder than anyone else every day. Now, they work hard."

Setting a Trend

College scouts were lining up to recruit Garnett. There was just one hurdle he couldn't quite get over—the ACT test. He tried four times, but he could not meet the minimum score required to play college basketball in Division I, where the most competitive teams play. The scholarship offers began to dry up. But Kevin was not ready to let his dream of playing basketball disappear.

Garnett, already standing 6 feet, 11 inches tall, instead chose to declare his eligibility for the NBA Draft. The last time a player had gone straight from high school to the NBA was 1975. Kevin Garnett had not even been born! While skilled and tall, he was young and inexperienced. As the draft approached, critics wondered whether the young player would be able to make it in the NBA.

The Minnesota Timberwolves decided to take a chance on Gar-

several times," Shirley recalled. "I cried many nights."

But their troubles seemed to evaporate when Kevin was playing basketball. During his senior season, he didn't let his bleak home life affect his attitude on the court. He earned the title of National Player of the Year by *USA Today* after leading Farragut to a 28–2 record. He was also named "Mr. Basketball" for the state of Illinois, averaging 28.2 points and 17.9 rebounds per game. Following that season, Kevin played in the prestigious McDonald's All-American game. Once again, he added to his trophy case—collecting Most Outstanding Player honors.

> *"I've always embraced the fact that there are going to be some difficult times, especially when you're dealing with change. I can only control what I do, so I go out and lace them up every night. I throw the hard hat on, the utility belt, and I go out there and give it my all."*
>
> —*Kevin Garnett*

Garnett, Kevin

nett, selecting him with the fifth overall pick of the 1995 NBA Draft. His first contract gave him $5.6 million for three years; the Timberwolves made the 18-year-old their franchise player.

All Eyes on the Rookie

Many eyes focused on Garnett during his rookie season. People were eager to see whether the high school star would be able to handle the physical play of the NBA. He averaged just over 10 points per game. He also chipped in an average 6 rebounds per game. He was awarded with NBA All-Rookie Second Team honors.

Although his rookie season was only average, Garnett vowed to improve. He worked hard in the off-season to increase his body weight and strength. He took hundreds of shots per day to improve his jump shot and increase his shooting range. And the hard work paid off.

Many believe that Garnett's success opened the door for more players to make the jump directly from high school to the NBA. Since Garnett's move in 1995, stars such as Kobe Bryant, Amare Stoudemire, and LeBron James have bypassed college to enter the NBA following high school stardom. But the NBA closed the

door in 2006. It now requires high school seniors to wait a year before becoming eligible for the NBA Draft.

A Star Is Born

Garnett nearly doubled his points and rebounds per game totals the following two seasons. He led the Timberwolves to their first-ever playoff appearance. For his efforts, Garnett was named to his first All-Star game in 1997. It would be the first of seven consecutive appearances dating to 2003. At the 2003 All-Star game, Garnett earned MVP honors by notching 37 points and 9 rebounds.

In 2000, he was selected for the U.S. Olympic Team. He and his fellow NBA stars captured the gold medal at the 2000 Olympics in Sydney, Australia.

Growing to Be a Leader

Garnett had proven that it could be done: He was a legitimate NBA superstar. "Many of us didn't quite know what to make of Kevin Garnett coming straight to the NBA from high school. But he has worked himself into the best player in the league," said John Rawlings, editor of the *Sporting News*. "He is not only the best player in the league but also the heart of the Timberwolves team."

Garnett's skills have translated into team success. The Timberwolves had a record of 21–61 in the season prior to drafting Kevin Garnett. Since Garnett's arrival, the Timberwolves have climbed to be among the elite of the NBA. Much of the success has been credited to Garnett, the undeniable team leader. His all-around play and positive attitude have inspired his teammates and coaches to reach new heights.

Garnett guided the Timberwolves to a 58–24 record during the 2003–04 season, establishing a franchise record. Minnesota finished atop the Western Conference standings, and Garnett led the league in rebounding (13.9 rebounds per game) and finished third in scoring (24.2 points per game). He collected the NBA's MVP award following the season.

Despite receiving the prestigious award, Garnett remained humble and focused. "I couldn't have done it without the support of my teammates, coaches, and you, the fans," Garnett explained after receiving the MVP trophy. "This award is a reflection of everyone's hard work and persistence. It's a great feeling to be recognized with the MVP award but this is a team game and the ultimate goal is to win the NBA title."

Sacramento Kings forward Peja Stojakovic (16) reaches in to intentionally foul Garnett (21) during the final minutes of Game 7 of their NBA Western Conference semifinal series.

Tough Times for the Timberwolves

In 2004–05, Garnett led the Timberwolves to a middle-of-the-pack 44–38 record. Tougher times came the next season, when the team stalled out in the midst of coaching changes, at 33–49, near the basement of the Western Conference. As hope drifted away near the end of the season, coach Dwayne Casey and the team management decided to sit Garnett more in order to give more playing time to younger players. At the same time, that strategy aimed at improving the Timberwolves' position in the next NBA Draft. Fans weren't wild about not seeing Garnett at his best, and there were times when the arena filled with boos. Said Casey, "The most important thing for me, as a coach, was the fact that Kevin was here for his teammates. He was in the locker room pulling for them."

Kevin Garnett's meteoric rise to the elite of the basketball world has left many in awe. Although his list of personal achievements is extensive, Garnett has earned a reputation for being unselfish and focusing on team efforts. However, events of the last few seasons have left even Garnett disheartened. He told reporters in early 2006, "I've always said I'll be in Minnesota as long as they want me. I don't think I can take another one of these rebuilding stages."

NBA legend Bill Walton observed, "Who would have ever thought that a high school player would come in and change everything? But here is Kevin Garnett, who came from nothing and all of a sudden has become as great a player as there is."

Further Study

WEB SITES
"Kevin Garnett." *NBA Player Profile.* Online at www.nba.com/playerfile/kevin_garnett/index.html (September 2006)
Official Kevin Garnett Website. Online at www.kevingarnett.com/4xl_archive.aspx (September 2006)

PERIODICALS
"High School Star Kevin Garnett Makes Himself Eligible for NBA Draft." *Jet,* May 29, 1995, vol. 88, no. 3, p. 50.
Thomsen, Ian. "Kevin Up: The Ever-Improving Kevin Garnett Emerges as SI's Player of the Year." *Sports Illustrated,* July 5, 2004, vol. 101, p. 94.

⏱ Gebrselassie, Haile

Haile Gebrselassie (1973–   ), distance runner, was born in Asella, Ethiopia. His name is pronounced HIGH-lee geh-brah-seh-LAH-see. When he was a young boy, he listened to the 1980 Olympic Games on the radio. That year, Ethiopian runner Miruts Yifter won two gold medals. At that point, Haile decided to become a runner. He started training seriously and kept it up for four years. In 1992, Haile's training paid off. He won two gold medals at the World Junior Championships. The next year, he won the first of four world titles at 10,000 meters. In 1994, he set the first of many world records.

When he was 22 years old, he was hailed as the greatest distance runner on earth. He lived up to his reputation by winning gold medals in 1996 and 2000. Known for his ever-present smile and love of competition, he moved to the marathon distance (26.2 miles) after the 2004 Olympics and, in 2006, ran the fastest time of the year.

Haile Gebrselassie smiled. During the 10,000-meter race, the longest track competition of the 1996 Olympics, the Ethiopian star watched as a succession of runners took turns in the lead. The pace seemed easy; the runners weren't threatening any records. Instead, they were running the 25 grueling laps of the rock-hard Atlanta track as if they were playing poker, waiting for someone to make a play.

The best runners, the Kenyan runners and Haile from Ethiopia, were waiting to see who would show his cards first. Who would make the big move to break the race open? Haile's supporters from Ethiopia were pounding African drum rhythms in the stands, and the Kenyans could not help but listen to them. As the runners' feet pounded on the track, the tension built.

Finally, just after the halfway point, Kenyan Paul Koech took the lead. He sped up to world-record pace. The three Kenyans embarked on their plan to run a team strategy—to speed up the race and burn the swift finishing kick out of Haile's legs. Why did Haile look so comfortable running behind them, a broad smile breaking across his face?

Early Life

By American standards, Haile Gebrselassie had a difficult child-

Ethiopia's Haile Gebrselassie celebrates as he crosses the finish line to win the gold medal in the men's 3,000-meter race at the World Indoor Athletics Championships in Birmingham, England.

Gebrselassie, Haile

hood. Yet the man who became known as the world's greatest distance runner never thought so himself. He grew up with nine brothers and sisters in a one-room *tucal*. (A tucal is a dwelling with walls made of mud and wood and a roof of straw.) They lived near Asella, a city in the central Ethiopian highlands. Haile lost his mother when he was a child. His father, a farmer, could be brutal at times. "Sometimes he beat us two times a day," said Haile, "sometimes three times."

Later, Haile felt his gift of speed came from his father. He recalled, "He was not a runner, my father, but he was quick. I always remember it was very difficult to

Career Highlights

Won four straight World Championships at 10,000 meters (1993, 1995, 1997, 1999)

Won two Olympic gold medals at 10,000 meters (1996, 2000)

World Champion at half-marathon (2001)

Won four gold medals at World Indoor Championships

Set 20 world records by the age of 33

escape from him when he was angry. If he wanted to beat us, he would always catch us. Even me, he could always catch me."

Like many Ethiopian athletes, Haile's birthdate is a bit uncertain. He has listed it as April 18, 1973. He first dreamed of becoming a runner when he and his family listened to the 1980 Olympics on their transistor radio. He wanted to emulate his hero, Miruts Yifter, who won the 5,000-meter and 10,000-meter golds. "I wanted to be famous," he said. The young boy set his mind on becoming the best runner in the world. But how could someone from such a humble place hope to win gold?

Haile started training every day. He would run the entire 6-mile distance to school each morning. Then, when classes were over, he would run 6 miles back home. He had no coach, but he had a natural gift. Running became a part of who he was. He developed a fluid, effortless stride. Spectators wondered about the unusual way he held one of his arms. As he became famous, reporters asked about this. His agent explained that his arm was crooked because he had always carried books during his early training.

Drive from Within

The road to the Olympics is never easy, but many athletes have the complete support of their families. For Haile, the opposite was true. His father discouraged running, feeling it was a waste of time.

Many great Ethiopian runners trained in the area, and Haile wanted to make his own mark. When he was just 16 years old, with no coaching, he entered a marathon in the capital of Ethiopia, Addis Ababa. He clocked a promising 2 hours and 52 minutes. His brother Tekeye, himself a world-class runner, gave Haile an old pair of racing spikes. Haile tried them, but they never felt right on his feet. He threw them out.

Finally, in 1992, he met Jos Hermens, a former world-record distance runner who had become a top agent. Hermens had been invited to Ethiopia by the track federation to help Ethiopian runners gain more international exposure. That year, at the age of 19, Haile traveled to the World Junior Championships in South Korea. There, he amazed everyone by winning both the 5,000-meter and 10,000-meter races. He had only been training seriously for four years.

Competing Against the Best

The next year, he competed in the 1993 World Championships in Stuttgart, Germany, against the finest adult runners in the world. He left with gold and silver medals. Quickly, he was becoming a force to be reckoned with. In 1994, with no global championships on the schedule, he decided to chase records. He traveled to Europe to compete at Hengelo in the Netherlands. There, he ran 5,000 meters in 12:56.96, breaking the world record. Only three days later, rival Moses Kiptanui from Kenya took that record away.

The competition in distance running still looked very stiff. No one was calling Haile a favorite for the gold medal in the 1996 Olympics in Atlanta, Georgia.

Then, in 1995, the world began to notice his continued improvement.

Though he stood only 5 feet, 3 inches, Haile became a giant in the sport. He made headlines in May by breaking the 2-mile world record (8:07.46). Then he chopped more than 8 seconds off the 10,000-meter record with his time of 26:43.53. After winning another World Championship gold at 10,000 meters, he set his sights on the 5,000 meters. Running in Zurich, Switzerland, in the prestigious Weltklasse Invitational, Haile lopped a stunning 10 seconds off the world record with his time of 12:44.39.

His father told a reporter, "I stopped telling him about the uselessness of running."

Records Mean More than Money

By the end of the year, Haile was hailed by many as the athlete of the year in the sport. He was also wealthy beyond his dreams, but money meant little to him. "As long as I make enough to be comfortable and feed myself, I'm happy," he said. He sent money home to support his family. A Mercedes that he had won at the World Championships in 1993 still sat in a garage in Ethiopia, with just 26 miles on it. Haile was too busy to learn to drive.

"Titles and records mean so much more than the money I can make. Zurich was such a fantastic feeling; how can money replace something like that?"

Gebrselassie, Haile

In 1996, he continued his pursuit of his one true goal: the Olympic gold medal. "I don't yet compare to other Ethiopian stars because I haven't won any Olympic medals. That's what is important to my country," he said. Not since the great Miruts Yifter in 1980 had an Ethiopian male won a gold medal.

Running with Confidence

At the 1996 Olympics, Haile knew what he wanted to do, and he believed in his heart that he could do it. He wanted the gold.

At the halfway point in the Olympic final of the 10,000-meter race, the Kenyan team opened up. Haile did not panic. Instead, he felt calm and confident. With six laps left, the great Paul Tergat, two-time world cross-country champion, sprinted out into the lead. This move left the rest behind—all the other runners but Haile fell away.

The beat of the Ethiopian drums in the stands accelerated. Tergat was just as determined as Haile to win the gold. He ran his heart out, but with a lap still remaining in the race, Haile flew by him. Fans looked on in disbelief! Haile had just run 6 miles, and now he was sprinting the last lap, opening up a 12-meter lead on Tergat. With the world watching, Haile achieved

his goal. He had captured his first gold medal.

The statisticians' eyes bulged when they did the math and realized that Haile had run the last half of the race in 13:11.4, a time that would have won all but one of the Olympic 5,000-meter races in history.

Running to the Top of the World

Haile ran his way to an unprecedented streak when he captured his third and fourth straight world titles at 10,000 meters in 1997 and 1999.

An astonishing 1998 campaign also bolstered his reputation. The previous summer in Brussels, Belgium, Haile had lost two of his world records. When Kenyan Paul Tergat broke his 10,000-meter mark, Haile congratulated him immediately. Then, referring to the next year's scheduled race in the Netherlands, he added, "I shall regain it in Hengelo."

The next June, Haile came to the Dutch stadium ready to run. That morning wind and rain made the outlook gloomy, but by evening, the weather had settled down. Haile churned away at a steady pace, running the first half with the pacemakers and much of the last

half alone. His time of 26:22.75 cut more than 5 seconds off the record. When asked whether he thought it might be broken soon, he answered modestly, "After all, the record was run by a man, not machine."

Twelve days later, he regained another record in Helsinki, Finland. This time, the margin was slimmer. He regained the 5,000-meter record, clocking 12:39.36 to slice a mere 0.38 second off the standard.

One More Gold?

In the months leading up to the 2000 Olympics in Sydney, Australia, a problem with his Achilles tendon made Haile wonder whether he could do it. He even questioned whether he should enter the Olympics. "At the last moment, I decided to come here and try," he said once he had arrived in Sydney. He defended his 10,000-meter gold in a historic race that saw him sprint to victory by the faintest of margins. When he crossed the finish line, he was just 0.09 second ahead of rival Tergat.

In the years that followed Sydney, some felt that Gebrselassie had lost his edge. A new generation of athletes was running just as fast as he ever had. At the 2001 World Championships, he only

earned a bronze. Two years later in Paris, France, he settled for silver. Then in 2004, at the Olympics in Athens, Greece, Haile tried to win an unprecedented third gold medal at the 10,000 meters, but he finished fifth.

Retirement, however, was the furthest thing from his mind. For years, the running community had speculated about what Haile could do in the 26.2-mile marathon. No distance runner in history had ever displayed the range he had done. His best time in the 1,500-meter race was 3:31.76, which translates to a 3:47 mile. His half-marathon time was 58:55. No runner had ever run so fast at so many distances. What would he do in a marathon?

How Was the Marathon Distance Set?

The marathon is a race that commemorates the feat of Pheidippides, an ancient Greek messenger. In 490 B.C., he ran 25 miles from the plain of Marathon to Athens to announce that Greek armies had defeated the Persians in battle. He collapsed and died after his mission. The modern marathon distance of 26 miles, 385 yards was established in 1908 when the Olympics were held in London. The course ran from Windsor Castle to the Royal Box in London—a distance of 26 miles, 385 yards. The distance did not become official until 1921.

Going the Distance

In 2002, Haile tried the distance for the first time as a world-class runner, clocking an Ethiopian record 2:06:35 to place third in the London Marathon. But at the 2006 London Marathon, a wet day dampened his hopes. Because he always raced on his toes, he was more vulnerable to slippery pavement than runners who landed on their heels. He settled for a 2:09:05 and ninth place.

Critics started murmuring. Was he washed up at the age of 33? In September 2006, he silenced them with his performance at the marathon in Berlin, Germany. He battled headwinds in the later stages and still clocked 2:05:56, just 61 seconds away from the world record.

Smiling All the Way

One thing that has distinguished Haile's career has been his smile and easygoing attitude. He is a man who genuinely loves to race, with all the excitement of a child going to the playground. Said his friend and manager, "He is an incredible talent. He's so relaxed—that's his strength....The smile at the start is genuine. He amazes me all the time how relaxed he is. He doesn't think a lot about tactics; he just runs and does his best and if someone is better, then they are better. No problem."

Further Study

BOOKS

Denison, Jim. *The Greatest: The Haile Gebrselassie Story.* Halcottsville, NY: Breakaway Books, 2004.

WEB SITES

"Biography: Haile Gebrselassie (Eth)," IAAF (International Association of Athletics Federations). Online at www.iaaf.org/athletes/athlete=8774/index.html (October 2006)

"Haile Gebrselassie," Ethiopia Athletes Web Site. Online at www.ethiopians.com/haile_gebreselassie.htm (October 2006)

FILM

Endurance [videorecording]. Burbank, CA: Walt Disney Home Video, Buena Vista Home Entertainment, 1998.

⚾Gehrig, Lou

Lou Gehrig (1903–1941), baseball player, was born in New York City. As a boy, he played football, soccer, and baseball. But before long, he turned his attention completely to baseball. Gehrig attracted the interest of the New York Yankees while he was at Columbia University. He dropped out of school to sign with them after his parents became ill. Gehrig had short stints with the Yanks in 1923 and 1924 and finally made the lineup for good in 1925. During his career that spanned 17 years, he played in 2164 games. But more remarkable was that he played in 2130 consecutive games, a feat that earned him the nickname "The Iron Man." His other major feats were equally impressive. In 13

of his 14 seasons, he drove in more than 100 runs. His American League record of 184 runs batted in during one season still stands. He hit .340 over his career. He asked to be taken out of the lineup in 1939 because of failing health. In 1939, Lou Gehrig was elected to baseball's Hall of Fame.

If there is one word that best describes Lou Gehrig, it is courage. He was a man who time after time came through with a hit in the clutch, who overcame countless injuries to play 2130 straight games during a 17-year career, and who would call himself "the luckiest man on the face of the Earth" on a day he knew he was dying. His performance record is outstanding, yet he meant more to the New York Yankees as a man than as a ballplayer.

In a history book on the Yankee dynasty from the 1920s through the 1950s, baseball historian Stanley Frank said of Gehrig, "Lou was not the best ballplayer the Yankees ever had...yet Lou was the most valuable player the Yankees ever had because he was the prime source of their greatest asset—confidence in themselves and every man on the club. Lou's pride as a big-leaguer brushed off on everyone who played with him..."

Prior to the 1937 World Series, Lou Gehrig takes a hefty swing during batting practice at the Polo Grounds, home of the New York Giants.

Gehrig, Lou

As valuable a player as he was, Gehrig did not receive all the praise he merited. There was someone else on the team who was stealing the thunder, someone who cast an awesome shadow—Babe Ruth. Yet Lou Gehrig never complained about being number two, though his personal relationship with Ruth was somewhat strained during most of his career. As number-two man, Gehrig was still appreciated for his talents. Even today, the names of Ruth and Gehrig are often linked together as the greatest one-two punch in baseball history.

Gehrig was also helpful in Ruth's legendary home run career. He hit in the cleanup spot behind Ruth. Opposing pitchers would often prefer to pitch to Ruth rather than walk him and face Gehrig with a man on base. They knew that Gehrig had a remarkable knack for driving in runs.

He played only 14 full seasons for the Yankees. Yet in 13 of them he drove in more than 100 runs, including (in 1931) an American League record of 184 in one season. Gehrig compiled a lifetime batting average of .340, hit 493 homers, drove in 1991 runs, and won four American League Most-Valuable Player (MVP) awards, something never done before. A member of the Hall of Fame,

"Today I consider myself the luckiest man on the face of the Earth."

—Lou Gehrig, in his farewell speech

Gehrig's mom and dad come out to the ballpark to see their son in action.

Gehrig was also voted baseball's all-time first baseman in 1969 by a panel of sportswriters.

Lou Gehrig was always at his best under pressure, as shown by his World Series records. In seven World Series (34 games) Gehrig batted .361, hit 10 homers, drove in 35 runs, and had a slugging percentage of .731.

The Yankees won 27 of those 34 games. Gehrig drove in the winning or go-ahead run in seven of them.

The Early Years

Born in New York City on June 19, 1903, Henry Louis Gehrig was the son of German immigrants. He was the only one of four children who survived the hardships of life in the new country.

His father was an ironworker when he could get the work. The family was so poor that young Lou had to take odd jobs after school to help with expenses. Yet he still found time for sports, excelling at football, soccer, and baseball.

When he was older, his parents were determined that he should go

Gehrig, Lou

again played a few games with the Yankees. He did well, hitting .500 for the handful of times he was up at bat. But he still needed game experience and was again sent to Hartford. That season he tore the minor league apart with a .369 average.

Gehrig still wanted the chance to get into the major league lineup. He was ready. He finally got his chance early in 1925. First baseman Wally Pipp reported to a game with a splitting headache

Career Highlights

Played in 2130 consecutive games

Holds American League record of 184 RBIs in one season (1931)

1927 American League MVP

Hit 23 career grand slams, a major league record

Held a career lifetime batting average of .340

Won the Triple Crown in 1934 with a .363 average, 49 home runs, and 165 RBIs

to college. Lou's mother took a job as a housekeeper and cook in a fraternity at Columbia University to help pay for his education.

After his high school graduation, Gehrig enrolled at Columbia. Finances still were tight and he waited on tables at one of the fraternities for extra money. Even then, with a job and classes to attend, Lou Gehrig found time to star for the baseball team.

He probably would have gone on to finish college, but both his parents became ill and Gehrig needed money badly. His baseball prowess then rescued him. The Yankees were impressed with his playing ability and offered him $1600 (the same as about $17,000 today) to sign with them. Gehrig took the money and left college for good.

The young pro trained with the Yankees in 1923, managing to get into 13 regular-season games before being sent to their minor league team at Hartford, Connecticut. The next year, he

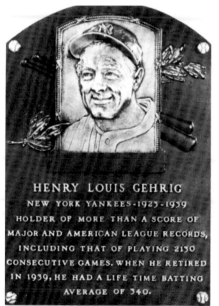

HENRY LOUIS GEHRIG
NEW YORK YANKEES · 1923 - 1939
HOLDER OF MORE THAN A SCORE OF
MAJOR AND AMERICAN LEAGUE RECORDS,
INCLUDING THAT OF PLAYING 2130
CONSECUTIVE GAMES. WHEN HE RETIRED
IN 1939, HE HAD A LIFE TIME BATTING
AVERAGE OF .340.

Henry Louis Gehrig was elected to the Baseball Hall of Fame in 1939, the year he retired. Normally, a player must be out of baseball for five years, but when voters learned that Gehrig was dying, they held a special election and Gehrig received the honor before his death.

the season, hitting 20 home runs and batting .295.

A Full-Fledged Star

The next season, Gehrig blossomed into a full-fledged star. It was not until 13 years and 2130 games later that he came out of the starting lineup. What took him out of the lineup was a fatal illness.

The illness that cut short Lou Gehrig's life at the young age of 37 began to show itself in 1938. He had won his fourth MVP award only two years earlier. He had a good season in 1938 with 29 homers, 114 runs batted in, and a .295 batting average. But it was not the kind of year the fans had learned to expect from him.

Still, no one suspected that there was anything physically wrong with "The Iron Horse," as Gehrig was called. Most thought it was just the wear and tear of so

after being cracked on the head by a pitch the previous day. Manager Miller Huggins gave Pipp the day off and put Gehrig at first base. Gehrig did so well that he remained in the lineup for the rest of

many straight games catching up with him.

Then, in the spring of 1939, the Yankee star began to suspect something was wrong. He suffered through a difficult spring training and managed only four hits in the Yankees' first eight games of the season. He then asked manager Joe McCarthy to take him out of the lineup for the good of the team.

When his condition worsened, Gehrig went to the Mayo Clinic in Rochester, Minnesota, for tests.

Gehrig as he looked on an early baseball card.

Gehrig, Lou

There he received bad news. He was suffering from amyotrophic lateral sclerosis (ALS)—a hardening and breaking down of the spinal cord (now known as Lou Gehrig's desease). There was no cure. The Mayo Clinic doctors said he would live only about two more years.

The Final Tribute

The baseball world was stunned at the news. The Yankees moved quickly to honor the man who had given so much of himself to the game for so many years. They proclaimed July 4, 1939, as "Lou Gehrig Day." During the pre-game ceremonies, they retired forever his uniform, number 4. A crowd of 61,808 turned out at Yankee Stadium to pay their final tribute to the Yankee hero.

Gehrig, who had given the fans so many dramatic moments over the years, gave them still one more with a speech that lives on as one of the most moving events in sports history. When he approached the microphone he was so choked up he couldn't speak. Silence fell over the stadium. An awkard moment passed and some-one moved to take the microphone away. But Gerhig stepped in, and then he spoke:

"Fans, for the past two weeks you have been reading about a bad break I got. Yet today, I consider myself the luckiest man on the face of the Earth. I have been in ballparks for seventeen years and I have never received anything but kindness and encouragement from you fans. Look at these grand men. Which of you wouldn't consider it the highlight of his ca-reer just to associate with them for even one day? Sure I'm lucky. . . . When the New York Giants, a team you would give your right arm to beat and vice versa, sends you a gift, that's something. When

New York Yankee manager Joe McCarthy (right) presents Gehrig with a trophy on behalf of the rest of the team on Lou Gehrig Day.

everybody down to the grounds-keeper and those boys in white coats remember you with trophies, that's something. When you have a father and mother work all their lives so that you can have an edu-cation and build your body, it's a blessing. When you have a wife

who has been a tower of strength and shown more courage than you dreamed existed, that's the finest I know. I consider myself the luckiest man on the face of the Earth. And I might have been given a bad break, but I've got an awful lot to live for."

The crowd sat stunned for a moment—then gave Lou Gehrig a thunderous standing ovation that brought the great player to tears.

On June 2, 1941, Lou Gehrig died, 17 days before his 38th birthday. He is remembered not only for his legendary feats on the field, but also for his inspiring strength of character. Lou Gehrig, "The Pride of the Yankees," stands as a heroic symbol in baseball history.

Further Study

BOOKS

Bak, Richard. *Lou Gehrig: an American Classic.* Dallas, TX: Taylor Publishing Company, 1995.

Hickey, David and Kerry Keene. *The Proudest Yankees of All: From The Bronx to Cooperstown.* Lanham, MD: Taylor Trade Publishing, 2003.

Macht, Norman L. *Lou Gehrig.* New York, NY: Chelsea House Publishers, 1993.

WEB SITES

Baseball Almanac. Online at www. baseball-almanac.com/players/ballplayer.shtml (October 2006)

"Lou Gehrig," *National Baseball Hall of Fame and Museum.* Online at www. baseballhalloffame.org/hofers_and_honorees/hofer_bios/gehrig_lou.htm (October 2006)

The Official Web Site of Lou Gehrig. Online at www.lougehrig.com (October 2006)

Gehrig gets a bear hug from Babe Ruth during Lou Gehrig Day in Yankee Stadium.

⊕Gibson, Althea

Althea Gibson (1927–2003), tennis player, was born in a rundown cabin on a cotton farm in Silver, South Carolina, and was brought up in New York's Harlem. Althea began playing paddle tennis on the city streets and later turned her attention to "regular" tennis. She won the New York State American Tennis Association (ATA) girls' singles championship in 1943 and the national ATA girls' title in 1945 and 1946. She then moved up to the women's ranks and won the national singles title in 1948. She defended that title for nearly a decade. Althea became the first African-American player in history to compete in a major national tennis tournament when she played in the national championships at Forest Hills in New York in 1950. The next year, she became the first African American to compete in

the prestigious tournament at Wimbledon. In 1957, she made more history, winning the Wimbledon and National singles titles. Following her tennis career, Althea Gibson turned her interest to golf and joined the Ladies Professional Golf Association (LPGA). In 1971, she was inducted into the International Tennis Hall of Fame.

Althea Gibson summed up her reasons for wanting a career in tennis when she wrote her life story and called it *I Always Wanted to Be Somebody.* She did indeed become somebody. Althea Gibson was the first African American in history to compete in a major tennis tournament. In 1950, she played in the national championships at Forest Hills, New York.

In 1957, she became the first African American to win a major tennis tournament when she captured the women's singles title of the All-England championships at Wimbledon. Then, in 1963, she broke the color barrier in women's professional golf.

Born in Silver, South Carolina, August 25, 1927,

After she became the first African-American woman in history to win the women's singles championship at Wimbledon, Althea Gibson was honored with a ticker-tape parade in her home town of New York City in 1957.

Gibson, Althea

Althea Gibson was the oldest of five children of Daniel and Anna Gibson, poor sharecroppers on a tiny farm. Unable to live on their small income, the family moved to New York City's Harlem district, where Althea grew up. At 13, she won several neighborhood paddle-tennis tournaments, including the Manhattan girls' championship, sponsored by the Park Department.

She joined the interracial Cosmopolitan Tennis Club with the financial aid of several of its members. There, she was coached by the club pro, Fred Johnson. At the Cosmopolitan in 1942, she entered her first tournament, the New York State Open championship. Although defeated, she was not discouraged. In 1943, she won the New York State American Tennis Association (ATA) girls' singles title. She took the National ATA girls' title in 1945 and 1946.

Althea's fine tournament play quickly began to attract attention. In 1946, she met two African-American doctors, Hubert A. Eaton of Wilmington, North Carolina, and R. W. Johnson of Lynchburg, Virginia. Both were interested in sponsoring the young tennis player. They especially wanted to break the color barrier at the Forest Hills tournament in New York, which until then had been exclusively white. She stayed alternately with the families of the two doctors, entering tournaments and graduating at last from high school.

In 1947, Dr. Johnson took her on tour and she won every tournament she entered. She even teamed with him to win mixed doubles tournaments. During this time she also met the boxer Sugar Ray Robinson, who became a close friend and offered encouragement throughout her career.

A Combination of Deftness and Power

Althea Gibson first took the national ATA women's singles title in 1948. She successfully defended the title for many years. Margery Miller Wells of *The Christian Science Monitor* wrote, "Her serve was remarkably like a man's, and her whole game was a combination of deftness and power..."

Becoming the first African American to play at Forest Hills in New York, in 1950, Althea Gibson is accompanied by former women's single champion Alice Marble. Althea had just won in the first round of the tournament.

Althea attended Florida Agricultural and Mechanical (A&M) University on an athletic scholarship (1949–53) and played on the tennis and basketball teams. In her sophomore year, she won the Eastern Indoor championship, sponsored by the U.S. Lawn Tennis Association (USLTA).

Finally, 1950 was the year she reached the goal set by her two doctor friends. Althea became the first African American invited to compete at the national championships at Forest Hills. A year later, she became the first African American to play at Wimbledon, England, although she did not reach the finals.

This setback seemed to begin a series of losses for Althea. By 1955, although rated eighth by the USLTA, she was so discouraged that she considered retiring.

Suddenly in that year, her tennis fortunes took a turn for the better. She met Sydney Llewellyn, a part-time tennis pro who believed Althea had a great future. Not only did he teach her new and winning techniques, but he also instilled in her a positive attitude. She began to tell herself, "You're going to win."

Althea Gibson was then chosen as one of four U.S. tennis players to go on a State Department goodwill tour of Southeast Asia. On the tour, she had many victories and gained valuable playing experience.

Wimbledon and Beyond

She defeated Angela Mortimer, 6–0, 12–10, to take the French women's singles championship. Then came a loss at Wimbledon in July 1956, her first defeat in 15 tournaments. But she teamed with Angela Buxton to win the doubles final at Wimbledon.

By 1956, the USLTA rated Althea number two, after Shirley Fry, among American women tennis

Gibson, Althea

Althea kisses the trophy she received for winning the women's singles title in the 1956 French International Tennis Championships.

players. She lost to Shirley several times that year, while defeating her only twice.

The year 1957 was Althea Gibson's greatest in tennis. In January, she teamed with Shirley Fry to capture the Australian doubles title at Melbourne. Seeding first at the July Wimbledon competition, Althea faced Darlene Hard of the U.S. in the finals. She was in complete control of the 49-minute match in 100-degree heat, taking the championship, 6–3, 6–2. The first African-American player to win the Wimbledon title, she also

teamed with Hard to capture the doubles title. Althea Gibson was congratulated by Queen Elizabeth and received from her the gold tray of victory. On her return to New York City, she was greeted with a ticker-tape parade, an honor shown to few sports stars.

In July, Gibson won the National Clay Court champion-

ships, her first major victory in the U.S. In August, she helped four teammates defeat the British team at the women's Wightman Cup tennis matches in Sewickley, Pennsylvania. The next month, she defeated Louise Brough, 6–3, 6–2, to take the national women's singles championship at Forest Hills in New York. Althea repeated her victories at Wimbledon and Forest Hills in 1958. She then retired from competitive tennis. "Shaking hands with the Queen of England was a long way from being forced to sit in the colored section

Defending women's singles champion Althea Gibson runs hard to return a shot during the 1958 championships at Wimbledon. She easily won the match.

"Shaking hands with the Queen of England was a long way from being forced to sit in the colored section of the bus going into downtown Wilmington, North Carolina."

—*Althea Gibson*

Althea turned to acting in the 1959 movie about the Civil War, The Horse Soldiers.

Breaking Down Barriers

LPGA director Lenny Wirtz helped Althea break down color prejudices in golf by insisting that tournaments accept all players in the association. Despite steady travel and hard work on her part, Althea did not find professional golf financially rewarding for a woman at that time. In her best year, 1967, she entered 25 events and earned only $5500 (or about $30,464 today).

Yet the lightning that struck at Forest Hills and Wimbledon in the 1950s opened the gates of tennis to all players, regardless of race. In 1990, 30 years after Gibson won at Wimbledon, Zina Garrison, another African-American woman, reached the finals. When Venus Williams won at Wimbledon in 2000 she paused to remember Gibson: "It had to be hard because people were unable to see past color," Williams said.

Gibson died of respiratory failure at a hospital in East Orange, New Jersey, in 2003 at the age of 76. "I am grateful to Althea Gibson for having the strength and courage to break through the racial barriers in tennis," Venus Williams said on hearing the news of her death. "Her accomplishments set the stage for my success, and through players like myself, Serena, and many others to come, her legacy will live on."

Further Study

BOOKS

Biracree, Tom. *Althea Gibson*. New York, NY: Chelsea House Publishers, 1989.

Cantwell, Lois and Pohla Smith. *Women Winners: Then and Now*. New York, NY: Rosen Publishing Group, 2003.

Davidson, Sue. *Changing the Game: The Stories of Tennis Champions Alice Marble and Althea Gibson*. Seattle, WA: Seal Press, 1997.

WEB SITES

"Hall of Famers," *International Tennis Hall of Fame*. Online at tennisfame.com (October 2006)

Career Highlights

Won the National Negro singles title in 1948 and defended the title for nearly 10 straight years

Won the Wimbledon singles and doubles titles in 1957

Captured the 1957 National Clay Court Championship

Inducted in 1971 to both the National Lawn Tennis Hall of Fame and International Tennis Hall of Fame

---

of the bus going into downtown Wilmington, North Carolina," wrote Althea Gibson the year she retired from tennis. Althea Gibson had reached her goal. She had become "somebody."

At 32, Althea Gibson was giving up tennis, but not sports. She became a pro golfer in 1963 by joining the Ladies Professional Golf Association (LPGA). After she had climbed to the top of the tennis world, she said, "There was seemingly nothing else for me to do. I wanted to stay in sports a little longer. I felt that if I was an athlete, I could do something else. Golf seemed the thing I could go into and make a contribution."

⚾ Gibson, Josh

Josh Gibson (1911–1947), baseball player, was born in Buena Vista, Georgia. He began playing sandlot ball at the age of 12. Gibson moved up in the semipro ranks at the age of 18, when he joined the Crawford Colored Giants in Pittsburgh, Pennsylvania. By 1931, he was a starting catcher for the famous Homestead Grays of the Negro National League. Although there are no official records, it is said that Gibson hit 75 home runs in the 200 or so games he played in 1931. The stars of the Grays, including Gibson, moved to Pittsburgh in 1934 and played for a team known as the Crawfords. This club is generally recognized as the greatest of the historic all-black teams. Gibson, who was fast gaining a reputation as "The Black Babe Ruth," returned to the Grays in 1936 and led them to nine consecutive pennants from 1937 to 1945. Gibson played 17

years in all and hit almost 800 career home runs. He led the Negro National League in batting four times, including highs of .457 in 1936 and .440 in 1938. In 1947, the year black ballplayers finally got a chance to sign major league contracts, Gibson died of a brain hemorrhage. He was enshrined in the Baseball Hall of Fame in 1972.

They called him "The Black Babe Ruth." Yet one of the great tragedies of baseball history is that the name Josh Gibson cannot be found in any major league record book.

Recognized by many as the greatest hitter who ever lived, Gibson was unlucky enough to have played before baseball's color bar-rier was broken. He never received the honor he was due.

Joshua Gibson was a legend in the Negro Leagues for 17 years. He died at the age of 35—only three months before Jackie Robinson became the first African-American player to play Major League Baseball.

Old-timers who remembered Josh Gibson—who batted right-handed with tremendous force—are convinced he had more power than Babe Ruth. Although records were seldom kept in the early Negro Leagues, Gibson is said to have hit 66 home runs in league play in 1934 (more than Ruth did). And he is believed to have hit the

In this rare picture, Gibson slips by the catcher to score a run during the 12th annual East-West All-Star Negro baseball game in 1944.

longest home run ever clouted at Yankee Stadium.

People who remember that legendary blast say the ball hit just two feet from the top of the stadium wall that circled the bleachers in center field—about 580 feet from home plate. It was estimated that if the drive had been two feet higher, the ball would have sailed out of the park and traveled an unbelievable 700 feet.

Babe Ruth's swing was awesome and his body wound up like a pretzel when he missed the ball. But Gibson's power was generated with little effort. He could hit every type of pitch with the same effectiveness.

"You couldn't trick him," Hilton Smith, a top reliever in the Negro Leagues, once recalled. "You just had to try to overpower him. He was some ballplayer. The minute you slipped, it was gone."

Better than Babe Ruth?

A muscular 6-foot, 200-pounder, Gibson was one of the first modern wrist-hitters. Besides being a power slugger, he was also an excellent hitter for average. In 1936, for example, he led the Negro National League with a .457 average. Two years later, he hit .440. Gibson was the Negro National League batting champion in 1936, 1938, 1942, and 1945. He blasted almost 800 home runs in league

and independent baseball. He was also a fast runner for his size and stole several bases each year.

"There's never been power like Josh's," the great Satchel Paige once said. "He wasn't just a slugger, either. He was a high average man, too. If I had to rate the top hitters, I'd put him ahead of Ted Williams of Boston, Joe DiMaggio of New York, and Stan Musial of St. Louis, and right in that order."

The hitter was also his team's catcher. There is a wide division of opinion among those who played with and against Gibson as to his receiving skill. Roy Campanella, a Hall of Fame catcher, played against Gibson for several years and claims that Josh Gibson was a

great defensive catcher. Others say that he was good—but not great. He had trouble with foul pop-ups.

"He didn't have the sure hands Campanella had," recalls Gibson's former teammate James Bell. "Josh dropped a lot of balls. But Josh was a smart catcher. He was smart and he was fast. Sometimes he just dropped the ball on purpose to get some guy to run. And he threw a light ball; you could catch it without a glove. Campanella threw a brick."

The Early Years

Joshua Gibson was born December 21, 1911, to Mark and Nancy Gibson in Buena Vista, Georgia, near Atlanta. He was the first of three children. When he was 12, the family moved to Pittsburgh.

Gibson, Josh

Josh began playing sandlot ball before he turned 13. He showed such talent that by the time he reached 16, he was starting for an all-African American amateur team in Pittsburgh.

Gibson quit school after completing the ninth grade in Allegheny Vocational School, where he learned the electrician's trade. To support himself, he got a job as an apprentice in a plant that made air brakes.

Career Highlights

Unofficially hit 75 home runs during the 1931 season

Once hit a baseball approximately 580 feet, likely the longest home run ever hit at Yankee Stadium

Led the Pittsburgh Crawfords to nine consecutive Negro League pennants from 1937–45

Hit nearly 800 career home runs

Led the Negro League in batting four times, hitting .457 in 1936

Enshrined in the Baseball Hall of Fame (1972)

In 1929–30, Gibson was catching for the Crawford Colored Giants of Pittsburgh, a semipro club. There he caught the eye of William "Judy" Johnson, then manager of the Homestead Grays of the Negro National League. Johnson himself was a standout third baseman for the Grays and knew a special talent such as Gibson's when he saw one.

Gibson had been gaining publicity by consistently banging 400- to 500-foot homers during the Giant games. Local Pittsburgh fans kept wondering why the Homestead Grays did not sign him.

The answer was simple. The Grays had two outstanding catchers in Buck Ewing and Vic Harris and had no room for another. But one summer night in 1929, Gibson got a chance to play for the Grays through a strange twist of fate.

The Kansas City Monarchs, the Negro National League champs of 1929, came to Pittsburgh for a series with the Grays. On the night of the first game, Ewing was hurt. Harris was being used in the outfield and Homestead needed a catcher to finish the game. Johnson spied Gibson sitting in the stands and sent the Grays' owner, Cum Posey, to fetch him. Gibson finished the game behind the plate and spent the rest of the season as a batting practice catcher for the Grays.

An Established Star

The next year Gibson became a regular outfielder and by 1931 he was an established star. That year he is said to have hit 75 home runs—although some were hit against semipro competition and were accomplished over a span of nearly 200 games.

In 1934, practically all the players on the Grays team jumped to Pittsburgh, becoming known as the Crawfords. That team was generally recognized as the greatest Negro League team of all time. Besides Gibson, Johnson, and the other Grays stars, the team included the legendary pitcher Satchel Paige. Gibson remained with the Crawfords for five years—his fame growing each season.

In 1936, the Crawfords disbanded. Paige went to the Kansas City Monarchs and Gibson returned to the Homestead Grays. In 1937, Gibson decided to play in the Dominican Republic, but he returned in July to help the Grays win their first Negro League championship.

"If I had to rate the top hitters, I'd put him [Gibson] ahead of Ted Williams of Boston, Joe DiMaggio of New York, and Stan Musial of St. Louis, and right in that order."
—Satchel Paige

JOSHUA (JOSH) GIBSON
NEGRO LEAGUES 1930-1946
CONSIDERED GREATEST SLUGGER IN NEGRO
BASEBALL LEAGUES. POWER-HITTING CATCHER
WHO HIT ALMOST 800 HOME RUNS IN LEAGUE
AND INDEPENDENT BASEBALL DURING HIS
17-YEAR CAREER. CREDITED WITH HAVING
BEEN NEGRO NATIONAL LEAGUE BATTING
CHAMPION IN 1936-38-42-45.

Between 1937 and 1945, the Grays dominated the league by winning nine straight pennants. Josh Gibson played a vital role in that success—with the exception of two years, 1940 and 1941, when he jumped to the Mexican League after being offered a larger salary. He earned $6000 a year playing for Vera Cruz (an amount which would be over $79,000 today), which was $2000 more than he had received from the Grays.

Gibson returned to the Grays in 1942 but staged a holdout, along with Buck Leonard, for more money. He settled for $1000 a month (about $11,000 today) and $1 a day for meal money. But he was not the same on the field as he had

Elected to the Baseball Hall of Fame in 1972, Gibson was never allowed to play in the major leagues. He died at age 35, just a few months before Jackie Robinson broke baseball's color barrier in 1947.

been before going to Mexico. On January 1, 1943, it was discovered that Gibson was suffering from a brain tumor.

Amazingly, he led the Negro National League in homers and batting in both 1944 and 1945, despite the tumor.

African Americans in the Majors

Usually fun-loving off the field and accepting hardships without malice, Gibson suddenly became bitter. The reason for his bitterness in the 1940s was that it seemed an African American was finally going to get a chance to play in the majors, and Josh Gibson knew he would not be that man. So, when young players such as Jackie Robinson, Roy Campanella, Monte Irvin, and Larry Doby of the Negro National League began to sign contracts, Gibson showed extreme frustration.

On the night of January 20, 1947, he went to his mother's home complaining of a headache.

A doctor was called to give Gibson a shot to help him sleep. A few hours later, while still asleep, he died of a stroke. The official report said Josh Gibson died of a brain hemorrhage, but most of his friends insisted that he died of a broken heart.

In the early 1970s, a committee was formed to honor former stars of the early Negro Leagues with a place in the Hall of Fame. Gibson was among the first to be honored. His name is now enshrined next to those of Babe Ruth, Jimmie Foxx, Lou Gehrig, and the other greats of his generation. The pity is that Josh Gibson did not live to see it happen.

Further Study

BOOKS

Brashler, William. *Josh Gibson: A Life in the Negro Leagues.* Chicago, IL: I.R. Dee, 2000.

Ribowsky, Mark. *The Power and the Darkness: The Life of Josh Gibson in the Shadows of the Game.* New York, NY: Simon and Schuster, 1996.

Twemlow, Nick. *Josh Gibson.* New York, NY: Rosen Central, 2002.

WEB SITES

Baseball Almanac. Online at www.baseball-almanac.com/players/ballplayer.shtml (October 2006)

"Josh Gibson," *National Baseball Hall of Fame and Museum.* Online at www.baseballhalloffame.org/hofers_and_honorees/hofer_bios/gibson_josh.htm (October 2006)

Gipp, George

George Gipp (1895–1920), football player, was born in Laurium, Michigan. He competed in baseball, track, and hockey as a youth, and also excelled in pocket billiards. He never played organized football until he arrived on the Notre Dame campus. Knute Rockne, the Notre Dame coach, discovered Gipp on a campus playground and invited him to try out for the team. Gipp did, and from 1917 through 1920 he was a star, leading the Irish to unbeaten seasons

in 1919 and 1920. In his final year at Notre Dame, he signed a baseball contract with the Chicago Cubs, but he never got a chance to prove himself. He contracted a throat infection just before the football season ended and died in mid-December, 1920. Rockne called Gipp the best all-round football player there ever was.

In St. Joseph's Hospital, South Bend, Indiana, a young man lay close to death on December 14, 1920. Gloom hung heavy over the nearby campus of the University of Notre Dame as fellow students and teammates knelt in prayer for his recovery. During the afternoon the youthful patient was baptized into the Catholic faith and received the last rites of the Church. Soon he lapsed into a coma. Three hours later George Gipp, All-American, was dead.

A young man of many talents, both on and off the athletic field, George Gipp was born in Laurium, Michigan, on February 18, 1895. With speedy legs and

an accurate throwing arm, he had been an outstanding basketball and baseball player during his high school days. But because of his frail build, he had shown little interest in football.

Dropping out of high school, Gipp had no plans for the future. Instead, he drove a cab and spent his spare time hanging around pool halls, becoming a pool and card shark in the process.

When he was 21, Notre Dame offered him a baseball scholarship. By chance, the famed Notre Dame coach Knute Rockne happened to spot Gipp booting a 70-yard punt. He challenged George to try out

for football. A few weeks later the new player startled crowds in Kalamazoo by dropkicking a 62-yard field goal against Western State Normal School to win the game.

George's first season was cut short by a broken leg, but in 1919 and 1920 the Irish of Notre Dame went unbeaten and were recognized as national champions.

Gipp's star never set. In the Purdue game of 1920, he made a spectacular run of 80 yards for a touchdown, only to see the play called back and Notre Dame penalized 15 yards. On the next play Gipp broke loose, sprinting to score on a 95-yard run.

His greatest game came against Army. His all-round play and his passes helped the Irish whip the Cadets, 27–17.

Gipp was also a sensation in college baseball. As a right-handed batter and centerfielder, he often smashed the ball beyond the 400-foot mark. The Chicago Cubs offered him a contract and he planned to play with them after graduation.

At 6-feet tall and 180 pounds, Gipp had good size but he did not care for the fierce body contact that is a basic part of football. Instead, he regarded it as a game of brains. When asked why he did not block and tackle more, he said, "I let the strong boys do that."

One teammate described Gipp's style of play as follows, "The thing that makes him a slick customer is that he avoids trouble. When he is hit with a solid tackle, he relaxes and goes down. He's always saving himself for the next time."

Off the field, school officials and Coach Rockne found Gipp hard to handle. For most of his school career he barely scraped through in his studies, even though he was highly intelligent. Studies did not seem important to him. Once he was even expelled for being found in an off-limits hangout in town.

Coach Rockne had trouble getting him to follow training rules. When he spoke to George on this subject, George casually remarked, "Aw, cut it, coach. You know I don't need to mess with that muscle stuff."

The immortal George Gipp as he looked during his playing days at Notre Dame in 1920.

His natural talent as an athlete was almost unbelievable. He ran like a racehorse. His passes were accurate and as swift as arrows. His punts seemed to be launched like powerful rockets. In 32 games, Gipp scored 21 touchdowns. In the last 20 games he played, he led Notre Dame to a 19–1 record.

However, the outstanding athlete was ailing before his last college game against Northwestern on November 27, 1920. He did not start but he later played a few minutes. A throat infection had set in and the miracle drugs of today had not yet been discovered.

Rockne was at his bedside shortly before he died. "I've got to go, Rock," he said. "It's all right. But, Rock, I want to ask one favor. Sometime, Rock, when the team's up against it, when things are wrong and the breaks are beating the boys, tell them to go in there with all they've got and win one just for The Gipper. I don't know where I'll be then, Rock, but I'll know about it, and I'll be happy."

Rockne first told the story eight years later during halftime when the Fighting Irish had limped into the dressing room locked in a scoreless tie with Army. There was not a dry eye in the locker room when Rockne had finished. The Irish then rushed out on the field to dump the Cadets, 12–6.

"How did you like that one, Gipper?" managed Rockne later,

as he raised his eyes above the field.

So, even in death, The Gipper seemed to be still winning games for Notre Dame, and Rockne dusted off the tale about every four years.

On the day of Gipp's death, Rockne informed his dying player that he had been selected by Walter Camp for his All-America team. He was the first Notre Dame player to win this honor. Years later, in 1951, he was elected to the College Football Hall of Fame. Nearly a century later, the legend of George Gipp lives on.

⊕ **Gordon, Jeff**

Jeff Gordon (1971–   ), racecar driver, was born in Vallejo, California. Gordon is one of the dominant stock car racers of his generation. He became the youngest champion of the Winston Cup circuit when he won the title in 1995 at the age of 24. Over a four-year span, Gordon won 40 races and claimed three Winston

Cup Series championships, a streak that placed him in the company of the greatest drivers of all time. Gordon totaled nearly $11 million in winnings during his 2001 points championship, a Winston Cup Series record. He is a three-time winner of the Daytona 500 (1997, 1999, 2005), the most famous stock car race in America.

Athletes often are asked for autographs in odd ways. But one experience might beat them all. Jeff Gordon recalls when a fan approached him by taking his shirt off. Underneath, on the man's bare chest, was tattooed a depiction of Gordon's stock car. "He asked if I would sign below so he could have that tattooed on as well," Gordon recalled in a 2003 interview. "It was very impressive to see the detail and size of his tattoo."

Signing autographs has come to be a regular part of Gordon's weekly ritual. As one of the most dominant and most popular stock car racers of his generation, Gordon has come to represent the best that high-speed racing on tracks of various types can offer. He preps

for a race with the utmost concentration and follows up with a variety of interviews. And then there are always the fans. They want his autograph: at the airport, in the racing pit, at the hotel where he might be staying—anywhere and everywhere he goes.

Gordon enjoys his success but takes it in stride. His strength and his success often seem as if they have come as a surprise to him. As he put it in a 1995 interview, shortly after rising to the ranks of stardom on the NASCAR circuit, "I'm just a kid. It's just a big blur, how fast I've gotten to this level. I can't even remember some things."

Jeff Gordon was born August 4, 1971, in Vallejo, California, a small farming community north

of San Francisco. He was barely a year old when he received his first exposure to racing. John Bickford, an auto parts maker and racing enthusiast, had invited Carol Gordon on a first date—to an auto race. Not sure what to do with her two kids, Carol brought them along. Bickford eventually became Jeff Gordon's stepfather, and he quickly gave the young boy an initiation into the joys of speed.

By age 3, Jeff Gordon couldn't get enough of going fast. He would race whatever vehicle he was capa-

Jeff Gordon (24) takes the checkered flag ahead of Ryan Newman, top, during the NASCAR Protection One 400 in 2002.

Gordon, Jeff

ble of propelling: a bicycle, a skate-board, roller skates. His mother often would worry, but she allowed her new husband to encourage her son's interest. When Bickford gave 4-year-old Jeff a BMX bike with the hope of helping the young boy get into bicycle motocross racing, Carol was horrified. "At BMX events they were hauling kids away in ambulances all the time," she recalled in a 1995 interview. After she forbade BMX bike racing, Bickford gave Gordon his first quarter-midget, a 6-foot car with a single-cylinder 2.85 horsepower engine. That small car became the vehicle that carried Gordon toward a career in car racing.

Career Highlights

NASCAR Rookie of the Year (1993)

Four-time Winston Cup champion (1995, 1997, 1998, 2001)

Youngest winner of the Daytona 500 (1997)

Tied with Richard Petty for the modern-era record for wins in a single season with 13 (1998)

Jeff would practice at least twice a week and race every weekend, traveling around the United States with his stepfather. Carol continued to worry. But she also had come to realize that her son had a special talent and was willing to let it be nurtured. Plus, she added in a *Sports Illustrated* article, "It didn't take long to realize that [the quarter-midget] was a lot safer than the bikes."

Gordon won his first quarter-midget championship at age 8. A year later, Bickford let him begin racing go-karts, which are race cars with small, 10-horsepower engines. Gordon began out-racing his competitors, most of whom were teenagers. Their families began to grumble, wondering about the fast, clean-cut boy. "All the other parents were saying Jeff was probably lying about his age, that he was probably 20 and just real little," Bickford recalls. "Nobody wanted to race us."

Gordon continued to race go-karts and quarter-midgets until he was 12. His career racing open-wheeled vehicles led to three national quarter-midget championships and four national go-kart titles. But Gordon wanted to try something faster. Working with his stepfather, he built his first sprint car: a 1,300-pound vehicle with a

650-horsepower engine. In California, he was legally too young to race a sprint car. But other states, mostly in the Midwest, did not have a minimum age requirement. After training with the sprint car series All-Star circuit in Florida for a year, the family decided to relocate to Pittsboro, Indiana. They saw the move as a way to help Gordon find races that would satisfy his thirst for speed and to move his racing career forward.

The family lived in pickup trucks and traveled from track to track. By the time Gordon was old enough to get a driver's license and drive legally on the road, he was a veteran driver at sprint tracks. He had won three sprint races and was racing full midgets, which are 925-pound cars with 320-horsepower engines. In 1987, when the U.S. Automobile Club (USAC) issued Gordon his racer's license on his 16th birthday, he became the youngest licensed driver in the history of auto racing.

He finished high school in Indiana as prom king and a cross-country runner. But racing had consumed his teen years. Often, he'd leave school early on Fridays or skip out altogether in order to race. By age 18, he began racing regularly on the USAC sprint car circuit, driving an 815-horsepower

open-wheel sprinter, as well as full midgets. He won the USAC Midget Series National Championship in 1990, becoming (at age 19) the youngest driver ever to claim that title.

At this point, his stepfather and mother suggested he take his racing to the next level and look into the National Association of Stock Car Racing, or NASCAR.

Love at First Sight

Stock cars are full-bodied cars. They're bigger and heavier than the sprint cars and full midgets that Gordon was accustomed to. However, he decided to attend a driving school run by a former NASCAR star, Buck Baker, in Rockingham, North Carolina, to see what the vehicles would be like.

It was like love at first sight. "That first day, the first time I got in a [stock] car, I said, 'This is it. This is what I want to do,'" Gordon told *Sports Illustrated* in 1995. "That car was different from any-

thing that I was used to. It was so big and heavy. It felt very fast but very smooth. I loved it."

For two years, Gordon shuttled between the USAC and the NASCAR tour. He continued to find success on the USAC circuit, driving open-wheel cars. In 1991, he earned the USAC Silver Crown Division National Championship and, for the second straight year, was named to the All-American team by the American Auto Racing Writers and Broadcasters Association. But he was faced with a dilemma. He could feel his passion changing. His heart was still into speed, but no longer the speed of sprint cars and full midgets. He had fallen in love with stock cars.

In 1991, Gordon teamed with car owner Bill Davis to form a race team for the Busch Grand National (BGN) division in NASCAR. In his first season on the BGN series, Gordon finished in the top 10 in 10 races and placed 11th overall in the season points standings. That

finish was good enough to earn him a Rookie of the Year award. In his second season, he earned $349,000 and won 11 pole positions. (The pole position is the number-one or best starting position for a race. Drivers compete in qualifying trials to earn their starting positions.) He also earned his first BGN victory in Atlanta, Georgia.

He returned to Atlanta in 1992. This time, his victory in the BGN series caught the attention of Rick Hendrick, the owner of one of the biggest, richest teams in the elite Winston Cup division of NASCAR. Hendrick recalls watching a white car cutting through turn after turn. As the white car pulled into victory lane, Hendrick asked "Who is that driver?" Somebody replied, "That's that kid Gordon."

NASCAR, unlike other racing circuits, draws much of its appeal from image. NASCAR drivers, especially those in the Winston Cup, race with numerous corporate

Gordon, Jeff

sponsors helping to pay the bills. Drivers with good looks, maturity, and strong public personas, along with athletic talent and driving skill, catch the sponsors' attention.

When Gordon and Hendrick met for the first time in 1992, Gordon was not quite 21 years old. Hendrick wondered whether Gordon could develop into a car racing superstar.

"Jeff had it all," he recalled. "It was just scary. He's good looking, and I couldn't believe how well he handled himself at age 20." Hendrick also feared that Gordon's good looks and talent would come with a dose of arrogance, making him too difficult to mold. Instead, he said, "What I found was a mature young guy who was kind of humble—a little bashful. A sponsor's dream."

A New Romance

Gordon signed a contract with Hendrick for the 1993 season. After finishing 31st in his first Winston Cup race in 1992, he earned the Rookie of the Year award in 1993. Then, in May 1994, driving a rainbow-colored Chevrolet, Gordon became the youngest man ever to win a Winston Cup championship. The victory came at the Coca-Cola 600 in Charlotte, North Carolina. Later that year, he won

the inaugural Brickyard 400 at the Indianapolis Motor Speedway. And he found a new love off the racetrack in Brooke Sealey, a Miss Winston model for that particular year. But NASCAR forbade drivers from dating Winston models, so Gordon and Sealey didn't become engaged until Sealey's season as a Miss Winston model ended. Gordon was 22 years old. His life seemed complete.

Over the next several years, Gordon dominated the NASCAR Winston Cup circuit. In 1995, he captured his first season points championship. He came up one spot short in 1996 but managed 10 wins and won the inaugural True Value Man of the Year Award.

But second was not good enough. He went out the next season and regained his standing as Winston Cup champion. His 10 victories that year included his first win at the legendary Daytona 500. During the 1997 season, Gordon notched his first road-course win at Watkins Glen, New York. In 1998, Gordon claimed another Winston Cup championship. On his way to the title, he posted 13 wins, a number that tied him with Richard Petty for the modern record for most wins in a season. He won his second Daytona 500 in February 1999, and after a flat

year in 2000, he bounced back to claim his third Winston Cup championship in 2001.

But as his victories mounted, his personal life faltered. In 2002, Gordon's wife filed for divorce. The turmoil that followed over the next 15 months affected his racing, leading to 31 straight losses over the year. He tried to stay calm, cool, and collected. But eventually he gave in and admitted to journalists that the personal issues were hurting his sport.

"I'm sitting there going, 'Oh, yeah, it's not affecting me. It's not affecting me,'" he told *USA Today* in July 2003. A few weeks after the divorce was finalized, he could only say, "I am so relieved to have it behind me."

Finding New Strength

Gordon was religious, and his interest in religion gave him a sense of strength after his divorce. He moved from Florida to New York, and gradually, his racing career bounced back.

He ended his winless streak in late 2002 with three NASCAR victories. Gordon returned to the top again in 2004 and 2005. He finished third in the Nextel Cup point standings in 2004 and won the Brickyard 500 for the fourth

Gordon displays the trophy in victory lane after winning the Busch Clash at Daytona International Speedway.

time in his career. In 2005, Gordon won his third Daytona 500. Called the "Great American Race," the Daytona 500 is the most prestigious stock car race in the United States.

Off the track, Gordon's personal life recovered and his image was restored. In 2003, he became the first NASCAR driver to host Saturday Night Live, a popular comedic television show. Then, in 2006, Gordon announced he was engaged to supermodel Ingrid Vandebosch.

As the winner of more than 75 Winston Cup victories, Gordon is among the top ten winningest drivers of all-time. Still, Gordon isn't satisfied. He observed, "Once you've got a championship, then your only goal is to win another one."

Further Study

BOOKS

Brinster, Richard. *Jeff Gordon.* Philadelphia, PA: Chelsea House Publishers, 1997.

Savage, Jeff. *Jeff Gordon: Racing's Superstar.* Minneapolis, MN: LernerSports, 2000.

Steenkamer, Paul. *Jeff Gordon, Star Race Car Driver.* Springfield, NJ: Enslow Publishers, 1999.

WEB SITES

24 Jeff Gordon. Official Web Site. Online at www.jeffgordon.com (October 2006)

♟Grace, W. G.

W. G. (William Gilbert) Grace (1848–1915), cricket player, was born in the village of Downend, in Gloucestershire, England. Growing up in a family of cricket players, Grace began developing into a first-class competitor in 1865. Before long, he became one of the best and most popular players in the game. Over a period of 44 years, he scored 54,904 runs, an average of 39.52 an inning, and 126 centuries (innings of 100 or more) in top-flight competition. As a bowler, Grace took a total of 2876 wickets in his career. Grace was captain of Gloucestershire for 29 years. During the 1871 season, Grace

scored a record 2739 runs. He also scored 400 not out in one inning of a game in 1876. Grace toured the United States, Canada, and Australia during his career. By the time he retired from first-class play in 1908, he had scored over 100,000 runs in both major and minor matches.

William Gilbert Grace—known throughout the world of cricket as "W. G."—was the first great popular hero of the game.

More than 100 years have passed since the lanky teenager first burst on the scene, but he still stands as the colossus of the cricketers. His personality and his example had as much influence on the game as his skill and his performances. Grace transformed

the art of batting in his lifetime. He set records that had been thought impossible. He astonished and delighted the fans at the same time. As a public figure, big and black-bearded, he was as well-known to Englishmen as was the prime minister.

Queen Victoria had been on the throne 11 years when William Gilbert (W. G.) Grace was born on July 18, 1848, in the small Gloucestershire village of

Downend, near Bristol. His father, uncle, and four brothers were all enthusiastic cricketers. Even his mother Martha had an unusual knowledge of the game and was an important influence on her sons.

In a regulation or championship match (game), two innings are played, with all players (11) on both sides having one turn at bat in each inning. A player remains at bat until he is put out. The match can often last for several days.

Something New for Cricket

When he was only 15, W. G. achieved the first of many victories for the South Wales Cricket Club against the Gentlemen of Sussex Brighton. The following year, 1865, he began in first-class cricket. By the time he was 18, everyone was calling him "The Champion." He showed a wonderful ability to combine defense and attack in his batsmanship, something cricket had never known before.

So expert was W. G.'s judgment of bowling, and so skilled his stroke-play, that unplayable pitches seemed not to exist for him. "He ought to have a littler bat," was the sad complaint of bowlers up and down England.

Fast bowlers especially were punished by W. G. without mercy. One, James Shaw of Nottinghamshire, remarked, "It is a case of I puts the ball where I please, and *he* puts it where he pleases." The better the bowling he faced, the better W. G. liked it.

W. G. Grace scored 54,904 runs at an average of 39.52 in nearly 1500 innings of first-class cricket over the remarkable span of 44 seasons. He was still a fierce opponent when he left first-class cricket in 1908.

Over the same period he also took 2876 wickets with his deadly round-arm style of bowling. This record alone would have made him an outstanding player. He also had great skill as a fielder. He served as captain of Gloucestershire for 29

W. G. Grace of Gloucestershire, England, is considered to be the greatest figure in cricket history. During his 44 years of play in first-class cricket, Grace scored 54,904 runs.

years. He also captained English teams in Test Matches at home and abroad. In regular matches of the Gentlemen versus the Players (the best amateurs against the best professionals), he always did well. In all matches, major and minor, he scored over 100,000 runs—a total once unapproached. Yet, with all his success, he never made an enemy. He kept to the end of his career a boyish zest for both cricket and life.

Another Record Broken

At 50, W. G. played his last Test Match for England after 21 previous appearances. Up to this time his career as a cricketer was a long, winning roll-call. Throughout the 1870s, runs flowed from his bat.

A huge man, his energy seemed endless. He set a new seasonal record total with 2739 runs in 1871 at what was then a remarkable average of 78.25. He again passed 2000 runs in 1873. At the end of this season, he married.

His honeymoon trip that winter was the first of his two visits to Australia. The previous year, in 1872, he had toured Canada and the United States with an English team under R. A. FitzGerald, Secretary of the Marylebone Cricket Club. On that tour, W. G. proved himself highly popular as well as

highly successful. He played at Montreal, Ottawa, Toronto (where he scored 142), London, Hamilton, New York, Philadelphia (where 21 wickets fell to him), and Boston. Altogether in the brief one-month tour, he made 567 runs, took 76 wickets, and held 22 catches. He also made after-dinner speeches that captivated his listeners on both sides of the border.

Another magic year for Grace was 1876. On July 10, he took a United South of England team of 11 to play a local 22-man team of Grimsby. The Grimsby captain complained that the side brought by W. G. was not strong enough.

The complaint turned out to be a foolish one. W. G. proceeded to make the highest score of his life in any class of cricket—exactly 400 not out in 13½ hours. He did this against 22 fieldsmen, 15 of whom tried bowling against the champion without success.

Grace, W. G.

His actual score was 399, but the scorers added a single to celebrate the mighty innings—and also the birth, on the second day of the game, of W. G.'s second son.

Just a month later, in August 1876, W. G. scored 344, 177, and 318 not out for a total of 839 runs in three straight innings in first-class cricket. Then, as now, this was extraordinary. Thousands of batsmen go through a whole career without reaching 300.

When he was nearing his 47th birthday, in 1895, W. G. became the first of very few players who have scored 1000 runs within the month of May.

Career Highlights

Captain of Gloucestershire team for 29 years

Scored 54,904 runs over a period of 44 years

Scored a record 2739 runs during the 1871 season

Credited with developing the modern game of cricket

In all matches, major and minor, he scored over 100,000 runs

When W. G. died, on October 23, 1915, England stood still for a moment in the midst of World War I to remember and to mourn "The Great Cricketer."

How Do You Play Cricket?

In Great Britain, cricket occupies the place held by baseball in America. Both sports are played with a ball and bat.

A cricket ball, hard and covered with leather, is between 8 and 9 inches in circumference and between 5½ and 5¾ ounces.

The bat, consisting of a flat surface for striking the ball and a round handle, can be no more than 38 inches long and 4¼ inches wide.

Cricket is contested by opposing teams of 11 players each, on a turf field, in the middle of which are placed two wickets facing each other at a distance of 22 yards. Each wicket consists of three round sticks, called "stumps," standing 28 inches high, with a distance of 9 inches between the two outer stumps. In grooves upon the top of the stumps lie two light pieces of wood called "bails."

The team at bat has a batsman at each wicket. The opposing team has a bowler at one wicket and a wicketkeeper behind the

The game of cricket has evolved tremendously since the 19th century and is widely played in both Europe and Asia. Here, a Pakistani batsman connects during a match against Sri Lanka.

other, with fielders in positions surrounding both wickets. The wicketkeeper corresponds to the catcher in baseball.

The bowler pitches, or "bowls," the ball, trying to place it so that, on a first bounce, it will strike the opposite wicket and dislodge a bail, so putting the batsman out.

The object of the batsman at this wicket is to protect it by striking the ball. A maximum of 6 runs are scored when a batsman hits the ball out of bounds on a fly. If a player hits the ball in bounds, both batsmen run to exchange places. If they succeed without being put out, a run is scored.

Sometimes, batsmen can run back and forth between the wickets and score several runs. During a run if a bail of a wicket is displaced by a fielder holding the ball, the batsman nearest the wicket is out if not within the popping crease (an area extending four feet from each wicket). The batsman striking

the ball is out if the ball is caught by a fielder before it touches the ground.

When a bowler has thrown six times, another bowler takes the ball and pitches from the opposite wicket. An inning lasts until ten players of one side have been put out. A game usually allows two innings for each team. Matches frequently last for two or three days.

Cricket is believed to have been played as early as the 1300s in England. The game's first rules appeared in 1744. By the 19th century, cricket had spread to England's colonies.

The modern game was largely developed by W. G. Grace in the late 1800s. International contests, called Test Matches, began between England and Australia in 1877.

The governing body for the sport of cricket is the International Cricket Council, started in 1909 and accessible online at www.cricket.org.

Further Study

BOOKS

Rae, Simon. *W. G. Grace: A Life*. London: Faber and Faber, 1998.

WEB WITES

"W. G. Grace," *Cricketinfoengland*. Online at Content_usa.cricinfo.com/england/content/player/13856.html (October 2006)

"The Ashes Tour: Ashes Legends XI," *BBC Sport*. Online at www.news.bbc.co.uk/sport2/shared/spl/hi/cricket/02/ashes/legends/html/grace.stm (October 2006)

⬤ Graf, Steffi

Steffi Graf (1969–), tennis player, was born in Brühl, West Germany. She asked to play tennis when she was only 3 years old. Her father sawed off the handle of one of his old rackets for the toddler to use. By age 13, Steffi was a professional tennis player. In June 1987, Graf won her first Grand Slam tournament, the French Open. Two months later, the 18-year-old was ranked number one in the world. Her forehand was described as the best in the history of women's tennis. In 1988, Steffi Graf won all four Grand Slam events—the Australian Open, the French Open, the Wimbledon championship, and the U.S. Open. She was the first woman since Margaret Court in 1970 to win the coveted Grand

Slam in a calendar year. Graf continued to win Grand Slam titles throughout the 1990s. She finished her career in 1999 with 22 Grand Slam titles. "Frauline Forehand," as she was known for her devastating forehand, held on to the number-one ranking for a record 377 total weeks.

Steffi Graf was 3 years old when she began playing tennis. Actually, she wasn't playing real, "by-the-rules" tennis. Her court was the living room of her family home. The net was a string tied between two chairs. She used a racket with its handle cut short because she wasn't big enough to use a standard-size racket. But the small girl displayed a big interest in the game of tennis.

At 3, Steffi was hitting tennis balls hard enough to break lights in the living room chandelier. At 18, she was hitting hard enough, and accurately enough, to be ranked number one in the world by the Women's International Tennis Association (WITA).

Steffi Maria Graf was born June 14, 1969, in Brühl, West Germany. (Germany was divided into two countries from 1949 to 1990.) Her father, Peter Graf, was an excellent soccer player and a nationally ranked tennis player. Her mother, Heidi, played tennis and helped operate the tennis club

Steffi Graf makes a forehand return during U.S. Open competition at Flushing Meadows, New York.

Graf, Steffi

Steffi Graf prepares to return a shot against Belgium's Sabina Appelmans during the 1991 French Open.

✪✪✪✪✪✪✪✪✪✪✪✪✪

The Record Book
Tennis (women)

Wimbledon singles titles, career

1.	Martina Navratilova	9
2.	Helen Wills Moody	8
3.	*Steffi Graf*	*7*
	Dorothea Lambert Chambers	7
5.	Blanch Bingley Hillyard	6
	Suzanne Lenglen	6
	Billie Jean King	6

Most singles tournament titles, career

1.	Martina Navratilova	167
2.	Chris Evert	154
3.	*Steffi Graf*	*107*
4.	Margaret Court	92
5.	Billie Jean King	67
6.	Evonne Goolagong	65
7.	Virginia Wade	55
8.	Monica Seles	53
9.	Martina Hingis	40
10.	Lindsay Davenport	38

Most Grand Slam singles titles, career

1.	Margaret Court	24
2.	*Steffi Graf*	*22*
3.	Helen Wills Moody	19
4.	Martina Navratilova	18
	Chris Evert	18

Records current as of November 2006

✪✪✪✪✪✪✪✪✪✪✪✪✪

that Peter purchased when Steffi was 8 years old.

It was at that tennis club that Peter Graf worked individually every day with his daughter. He felt strongly that Steffi should develop her own strengths instead of mimicking the playing styles of other champions.

Outsiders sometimes criticized Peter's devotion to Steffi's career. Steffi and her father looked at it differently. Both said his protection and guidance helped Steffi and enabled her to do her best.

Steffi was 3 years old when she won her first reward—a Pepsi—from her father for hitting the ball over the "net" in her living room. She was 6 when she won her first junior tournament.

The German Junior Champion

By the age of 13, she had won the German junior championship in the 18-and-under division and decided to turn professional. Steffi quit school, but she continued her education with a tutor. She became the second-youngest player ever to receive an international ranking. The WITA computer ranked Graf the 214th-best player in the world.

At the 1984 Summer Olympics in Los Angeles, tennis was played as an exhibition sport. The youngest player on the Olympic courts was 15-year-old Steffi. The best player on the courts was also Steffi, who took home the gold medal.

In 1985, Graf beat number-four seed Pam Shriver at the U.S. Open. The same year, Graf came in second to Martina Navratilova in a nationally televised tournament in Fort Lauderdale, Florida. The 16-year-old Graf could not contain her disappointment and ran off the court instead of attending the official ceremonies to present the trophies and prize money. Steffi ended 1985 without a single tournament win.

The next year, 1986, Graf was a little older, a little more mature, and a lot more pleased with her performance on the tennis court. She had eight tournament wins in 14 tries. She did not win a Grand Slam tournament, but she did have her first victories over Navratilova and Chris Evert.

But Steffi was still number three. She had improved dramatically from her number-22 ranking at the end of 1984. Still, what she really wanted was to be number one in the world. Early in 1987, she became number two.

Since 1978, Navratilova and Evert had been the top two women in the tennis world. Steffi Graf, the 5-foot, 8-inch, 17-year-old blond, beat both women in straight-set matches at the Lipton International Players Championships in early 1987. It was the first time Navratilova and Evert had both been defeated in straight sets at the same tournament since the late 1970s. Graf was making the two great women tennis champs notice that their 30th birthdays had come and gone.

At Last, A Grand Slam Victory

In June 1987, Graf won her first Grand Slam singles title when she defeated Navratilova at the French Open. Graf's talents were evident as she took the final, 6–4, 4–6, 8–6, to become the youngest women's champion in the tournament's history. A week later, Steffi turned 18. Two months later, Steffi moved to the top position in the rankings.

Graf finished 1987, her fifth year on the tour, with 11 tournament victories and a 75–2 record. Up to that time, only Martina Navratilova had ever had a better year (16 tournament victories, 86–1 record) on the women's tennis tour during the Open era, which began in 1968.

The first Grand Slam event of 1988, the Australian Open, was

Graf, Steffi

another victory for Steffi Graf. Her forehand, so powerful and precise, was helping to keep her solidly in the number-one spot.

One opponent commented, "I've played Martina. I've played Chris. Nobody hits the ball as hard as Steffi does." And that was what the tennis-loving Graf wanted to do. "I want so much to hit it hard and have it go in," she said.

Breaking Records

She did exactly that in the French Open in June of 1988. Graf's 6–0, 6–0 victory made her the first woman in the history of the

Career Highlights

Won the women's Grand Slam and an Olympic gold medal in 1988 at age 19

Captured three of the four major tournaments in 1993, 1995 and 1996

Won 22 Grand Slam singles titles, the third most in history

Retired in 1999 as third all-time with 107 career singles titles

Ranked as the number one player in the world for a record 186 consecutive weeks

tournament to become champion without giving up a single game.

Her victory also meant she had two Grand Slam events to her credit in 1988. She had a chance to win all four Grand Slam tournaments in a calendar year. No one had done that since Margaret Court 18 years earlier in 1970. Navratilova had won the Grand Slam tournaments in succession, but not in the same calendar year.

Steffi was hoping to move one step closer to winning the Grand Slam with a victory at Wimbledon in July. But Martina Navratilova was hoping just as hard to make history at Wimbledon. For her, victory would mean seven straight singles titles.

In the women's final at the famed tournament, Graf defeated Navratilova with a dazzling display of tennis talent. Steffi took the match, 5–7, 6–2, 6–1.

Steffi's quick feet, superior court coverage, and stinging forehand were matched by her drive and determination. Said tennis great Billie Jean King, "Her intensity is perfect, and that is what makes her a champion."

Graf had only one Grand Slam tournament left to conquer—the U.S. Open in September. In the

final, she met Gabriela Sabatini, the only player who had beaten Graf in 1988. Graf won, 6–3, 3–6, 6–1, and became only the fourth player in tennis history to win all four Grand Slam tournaments in a calendar year. (The others are Donald Budge, who won the Grand Slam in 1938; Maureen Connolly, in 1952; Rod Laver, in 1962 and 1969; and Margaret Court, in 1970.)

Olympic Gold and Wimbledon

She turned her feat into a "golden" Grand Slam at the 1988 Olympics. Representing West Germany, she won the gold medal in women's singles.

The next year, 1989, Graf won three legs of the Grand Slam—the Australian Open, Wimbledon, and the U.S. Open. She defeated Martina Navratilova for her Wimbledon and U.S. Open victories. Steffi also captured the 1989 Virginia Slims championship. In all, she won 14 tournaments and posted an incredible 86–2 record.

From June 1989 to May 1990, Graf won 66 consecutive matches. An injured thumb and family problems resulted in a subpar year for Steffi in 1990. Yet she remained number one. She finally fell from the top spot in March 1991. She had been the top-ranked player

ranked number one in the world—331 nonconsecutive weeks—than any other player in history. During the 1999 season, Steffi Graf decided that that season would be her last on the professional tour.

In October 2001, Graf married Andre Agassi. The couple lives in Las Vegas, Nevada, with their son, Jaden Gil, born in October 2001, and daughter Jaz Elle, born in October 2003. Graf, with Stefan Edberg and Dorothy Cheney, was named to the International Tennis Hall of Fame ballot for induction during the 50th anniversary celebration at the Hall of Fame in July 2004.

Further Study

BOOKS

Brooks, Philip. *Steffi Graf, Tennis Champ.* New York: Children's Press, 1996.

Knapp, Ron. *Sports Great Steffi Graf.* Springfield, NJ: Enslow Publishers, 1995.

McMane, Fred and Cathrine Wolf. *Winning Women.* New York: Bantam Books, 1995.

WEB SITES

"Steffi Graf," *Sports Illustrated Woman.* Online at sportsillustrated.cnn.com/ siforwomen/top_100/14/ (October 2006)

for 186 straight weeks—from August 17, 1987 until March 10, 1991—longer than anyone (man or woman) in history. Just when some were beginning to say that Steffi Graf had seen her best days, she won her third Wimbledon championship in 1991.

Steffi played one of her greatest tournaments at Wimbledon in 1992. Despite struggling to win against unseeded players in third- and fourth-round matches, she reached the finals against Monica Seles—the number-one player in the world. Once there, Graf crushed Seles, 6–2, 6–1, in only 58 minutes to win her fourth title at Wimbledon.

Through the end of 1999, Graf would garner seven Wimbledon titles, five U.S. Open titles, six French Open titles, and four Australian Open titles. She was one of the most dominating and successful women tennis players of all-time with her 22 career Grand Slam titles. She spent more time

⬤Granato, Cammi

Cammi Granato (1971–   ), hockey player, was born March 25, 1971, in Downers Grove, Illinois. Cammi is one of the world's best known female hockey players. She began playing hockey with a boys' team at age 5. She continued with the sport through high school. She attended Providence College on a hockey scholarship. Granato joined the newly formed U.S. women's national team, Team USA, in 1990. The team played in the Women's World Championship in 1990, 1992, 1994, and 1997. Granato was captain of the U.S. team when women's hockey became an Olympic sport for the first time in 1998. Team USA defeated Canada in the Olympic finals to earn the first Olympic gold medal.

The team followed that victory with a silver medal in the 2002 Olympics in Salt Lake City, Utah. Following the Olympics, Granato played professional hockey with the Vancouver Griffins, the team she joined in 2002. She currently serves as a television reporter for National Hockey League (NHL) games.

Cammi Granato stood on the top step of the awards platform at the 1998 Winter Olympic Games. The other members of the U.S. women's hockey team surrounded her. A gold medal hung around each player's neck. The medals were the first Olympic gold medals ever awarded to women in hockey. As the American national anthem played, Granato cradled the medal around her neck.

Tears filled her eyes. Her mind went back to another victory, 18 years earlier. The U.S. men's hockey team had taken the gold medal in the 1980 Olympics. They defeated the former Soviet Union in a stunning upset. Granato had watched the match as a child. A documentary, *Miracle on Ice,* told the story of that victory. It was one of her favorite films. Granato's mind also went back to the 1988 Olympic Games. Her brother Tony

Granato had been on the U.S. hockey team that year.

Now she was at the Olympics as a competitor and a winner. She was the co-captain of a team that had made history. Standing on

---

Cammi Granato (21), pumps her fist after registering a goal against Sweden during the 2002 Winter Olympics in Salt Lake City.

Granato, Cammi

the Olympic podium, she felt like a kid—the same precocious kid who had played hockey with the boys; the same optimistic kid who had wanted, some day, to win an Olympic medal. "It's funny thinking back on it now," she told the *Rocky Mountain News*. "But I didn't know until [I won one] that you got to keep the medals."

Power and Puck

Catherine Michelle Granato was born March 25, 1971, in Downers Grove, Illinois. She was the fifth of six children. She had three older brothers. All three boys, as well as her sister Christina, liked sports. In the winter, they especially liked hockey. They would flood their backyard with water. After a thick sheet of ice formed, they would rush out with hockey sticks, pucks, and skates for a family game. By the time she was 5 years old, Cammi was on the ice with her brothers and sister. She got her first coaching advice from her brother, Tony. Tony would grow up to become a star player in the NHL and, eventually, coach of the Colorado Avalanche. "We were going outside to play, and Tony pulled me aside," Cammi recalled in a 2004 interview. "He told me, 'If you get hurt, you can't tell mom.'"

"Mom" was Natalie Granato, daughter of a former minor league baseball player. She was happy to see her youngest daughter's enthusiasm for sports. But she felt that figure skating would be a more appropriate activity for a little girl. So she bought Cammi a pair of figure skates and signed her up for lessons. She drove Cammi to the small studio rink where skaters learned graceful, intricate moves. Cammi went along with the idea, until her mother turned her back. Then, Cammi would sneak out of her figure skating lesson. She ran next door to the larger rink where her brothers were playing hockey.

"I knew I was too clumsy to ever do a double axel," Granato told *Rocky Mountain News* reporter Steve Trivett. Cammi was better at hockey.

Her mother eventually agreed. Cammi obediently tried figure skating for a year. Finally, her mother gave in—and let her switch to hockey. For the next several years, Cammi played hockey with the boys' team, the Downers Grove Huskies. When she started high school, she played on a hockey team that had both boys and girls. She also played basketball, volleyball, tennis, and soccer. But hockey was her first love.

Hockey was a passion that Cammi's family fully encouraged. Her parents took the children to hockey camps for vacations. The Granatos read hockey books when they were assigned a book report for school. "You go to school, you play hockey, you watch hockey and you read about hockey. That's just the way it was for us growing up," Tony Granato recalled. But the sport held a future for boys. For girls, it did not. Still, Cammi Granato continued to play.

Cammi was not afraid to play rough hockey. As a member of the boys' team, she played whatever position was open. She loved playing too much to be particular about what position she played. Playing with the boys helped Cammi develop her talent for hockey. It also helped mold her into a women's sports pioneer.

"I didn't understand at the time that Cammi playing with the boys was out of the ordinary," Tony Granato told the *Rocky Mountain News* in 2004. "I think all athletes are like that—women's basketball, whatever—they had to be the pioneers for the rest of the groups that came after them. The girls that went through it … set the table for making women's sports not only acceptable but fun to watch."

Cammi Granato helped Team USA to the first Olympic medal in women's ice hockey at the 1998 Games in Nagano, Japan.

Clearing a New Path

After high school, Cammi Granato received a scholarship to play hockey with Providence College. Providence was an ice hockey powerhouse. Granato became the school's top scorer and its all-time leading scorer. For female hockey players in the late 1980s and early 1990s, playing college hockey was the highest level they could achieve. Women's hockey was not yet an Olympic sport, and there was no professional league in the United States to advance to.

In college, Granato didn't see herself as an exceptional player. The bigger star was her brother, Tony, who had become an NHL star. During her freshman year, 1989–90, Granato pinned up a poster of her brother on her dorm wall. For most of that first year, Cammi's roommate had no idea that the athlete on the poster was Cammi's brother.

As Cammi continued to shine on the ice, she began making news all on her own.

"At times … she felt guilty getting all the attention," her roommate—and teammate—Michelle Johansson told sportswriter Michael Farber. "She thought it was because she was Tony's sister, and it made a cute story. I had to tell her, 'Tony didn't score all those goals for you.'"

It was obvious to Johansson and her teammates that Cammi was an extraordinarily gifted player—even if she didn't realize it herself. But being gifted was not enough. After college, opportunities to play were limited. If Cammi wanted to continue playing hockey, she would have to chart a new course.

Cammi did just that. A year after she began college, Granato became a founding member of

Team USA. It was the first national women's hockey team. The fledgling team quickly became a powerhouse within the small circle of women's hockey. Team USA played in the world championships four times in the 1990s and in 2000 and 2001. Each time the team fell short of a gold medal, losing to number-one-ranked Canada.

But the first seeds were sown. American sports fans began to see women's hockey as a legitimate, exciting sport. Granato graduated from Providence College in 1993. She then went on to play at Concordia University in Montreal, Canada, where she was pursuing a graduate degree. She also continued to train with Team USA. By the late 1990s, she was ranked the fifth-best female player in the world.

Many male hockey stars rely on brute force and strength. Cammi's style of play was slower, more

Granato, Cammi

controlled, and subtler. She was no longer "Cammi Granato, Tony Granato's sister." She had become "Cammi Granato, premier American women's hockey player."

Yet this didn't mean much. Her brother Tony was offered a three-year, $4.5 million contract to play professional hockey. Cammi Granato was riding buses and sharing motel rooms. Women's hockey drew no more than a few hundred people to watch the game. And she was doing this not in the United States, but in Canada. Opportunities for women to play professionally in the United States were limited. In 1997, a men's team, the New York Islanders, invited her to try out. Granato chose not to. By then, she had a larger goal in mind: the 1998 Winter Olympics.

Going for Gold

Nearly every athlete dreams about the Olympics. Granato had been in the stands when her brother Tony played with the U.S. hockey team in the 1988 Games in Calgary, Canada. "The Olympics became so real for me when the athletes walked into that stadium in Calgary," she told sportswriter Farber. "The whole world comes to one place." The whole world is focused on the game.

Cammi thought about the magic of seeing the "whole world come to one place." If the entire world was watching women play hockey, Granato thought, perhaps women's hockey would gain the acceptance it needed. Women's hockey could become a legitimate sport. And, if the Americans could upset the Canadians, perhaps another "miracle on ice" could occur.

Ten years later, in 1998, the entire world watched the dream unfold. Team USA defeated Canada and won the gold medal. Granato's entire family was in the spectator stands, watching. The hockey-crazy Granatos were as excited and proud as a family could be. At the closing ceremonies, Granato led the American contingent, carrying the U.S. flag.

Over the next few years, Granato's dream started to become real. Women's hockey became accepted in the United States. More and more girls began playing hockey. And Granato was seen as the guiding force. Her picture appeared on a Wheaties box. Stories about women's hockey focused on her. At the 2002 Winter Olympics in Salt Lake City, Utah, Granato carried the Olympic torch up the steps to the point where the flame was lit.

Cammi Granato (middle) poses with Vancouver Griffins teammates Natalie Christenson (left) and Julia Berg (right).

Building a Future

Granato channeled her success back into her sport. She teaches hockey in Vancouver, Canada, and she began playing with the Vancouver Griffins in 2002. She and her brother Tony run the Cammi Granato Gold Medal Hockey Clinic for Girls. And, with the support of her family, Cammi organized the Gold Dreams for Children Founda-

Career Highlights

Played boys' hockey until her junior year in high school

Named MVP at the 1992 World Championships

Set career scoring records at Providence College: 256 career points, 99 goals, and 117 assists

Played more than 150 games for Team USA

Won first-ever women's hockey gold medal at 1998 Olympics

Carried torch at 2002 Olympics

tion to help children with special needs.

As of 2004, Granato was the oldest female hockey player in the United States. Nevertheless, she continued to play with Team USA.

Following the 2002 Olympics, Granato was one of three American players affiliated with a Canadian team, the Vancouver Griffins. But the Canadian league, the National Women's Hockey League, wants the teams to recruit Canadian players first. That means that opportunities remain limited for the growing number of young women hockey players in the United States—women who, like Cammi Granato, pick up a hockey stick and skates and play the sport for the sheer joy of it.

"We need to establish a post-college women's professional league in the United States," Granato told the *Rocky Mountain News* in January 2004. "We need to provide a place for girls to play once they are out of college."

A Disappointing End

Granato prepared herself for the 2006 Olympics despite her age. Players looked to her leadership and experience to improve their own games. However, Cammi was faced with a harsh disappointment. Prior to the Olympics, she was told she had been cut from the team and wouldn't be part of the Olympic roster. Cammi was devastated.

"I feel an overwhelming sadness," Granato explained. "I have a big, loving family and a roster full of former teammates that I love and respect. But, I'm so heartbroken right now. I could never fathom this is how my hockey career would end."

Without Granto leading the way, Team USA struggled. For the first time ever, the United States was defeated by a team other than Canada. The Americans took home the bronze medal, but many believed Granato's presence could have helped them win the gold.

A New Chapter

Granato now serves a television reporter for NHL games. She married Ray Ferraro, a former NHL player who also serves as a hockey commentator. With her expertise of the sport, it seemed like a perfect fit.

"It seems natural to me to be able to analyze what the players are doing," Granato explained. "I think I can offer a lot on TV."

While Cammi hasn't ruled out playing again in the future, she will remain a key figure in hockey, whether it be on the ice as a player, in the pressbox as a reporter, or in the box as a coach.

Further Study

BOOKS AND ARTICLES

Farber, Michael. "Ice Queen," *CNN/ Sports Illustrated,* 1998.

Loverro, Thom. *Cammi Granato, Hockey Pioneer.* Minneapolis: LernerSports, 2000.

Michaelis, Vicki. "Granato's Dreams Have No Age Limit," *USA Today,* January 9, 2004.

Trivett, Steve. "A Thirst for Ice has Fueled Cammi Granato," *Rocky Mountain News,* January 3, 2004.

WEB SITES

"Cammi Granato," *U.S. Olympic Team.* Online at www.usolympicteam.com/26_ 1166.htm (October 2006)